D0172235

A Perfect Match

GIRLS ONLY (GO!)

Dreams on Ice
Only the Best
A Perfect Match

GIRLS **GO** ONLY!

A Perfect Match

BEVERLY LEWIS

BETHANY HOUSE PUBLISHERS
MINNEAPOLIS, MINNESOTA 55438

A Perfect Match
Copyright © 1999
Beverly Lewis

Cover illustration by Paul Casale
Cover design by the Lookout Design Group

All rights reserved. No part of this publication may be reproduced, stored in a retrieval system, or transmitted in any form or by any means—electronic, mechanical, photocopying, recording, or otherwise—without the prior written permission of the publisher and copyright owners.

Published by Bethany House Publishers
A Ministry of Bethany Fellowship International
11400 Hampshire Avenue South
Minneapolis, Minnesota 55438
www.bethanyhouse.com

Printed in the United States of America by
Bethany Press International, Minneapolis, Minnesota 55438

ISBN 0–7642–2060–8

For

Heidi Koleto,

who ice-dances with her brother, Justin,
and has high hopes for the Olympics.

AUTHOR'S NOTE

Great, big thank-yous to Justin and Heidi Koleto—brother/sister ice dancers who happen to be homeschoolers!—and their mother, Michelle, for answering so many questions about the sport.

I am also grateful to the U.S. Figure Skating Association and the helpful folks at the World Arena in Colorado Springs, Colorado. My appreciation for the research assistance received from the IOC (International Olympic Committee).

For readers interested in learning more about skating news, tips, and the Stars on Ice tour, check out the Kristi Yamaguchi Web site.

BEVERLY LEWIS is the bestselling author of over fifty books, including the popular CUL-DE-SAC KIDS and SUMMER-HILL SECRETS series, and her adult fiction series, THE HERITAGE OF LANCASTER COUNTY. Her *Cows in the House* picture book is a rollicking Thai folktale for all ages. She and her husband have three children, as well as two snails, Fred and Fran, and make their home in Colorado, within miles of the Olympic Training Center, headquarters for the U.S. Olympic Committee.

 CHAPTER 1

"It seems like forever since our last club meeting," said Heather Bock. She sat cross-legged on the floor in Jenna Song's attic bedroom, holding the "minutes" notebook.

"I know what you're saying," agreed Jenna, residing president of the exclusive *Girls Only* club. "Christmas break was just too long this year."

Olivia Hudson—vice-president—spoke up. "Two weeks and two days, to be exact."

Jenna snickered. "Leave it to Livvy to count the days."

"Want the hours and minutes, too?" Livvy teased.

"No, thanks," replied Heather, grinning at both girls.

"It's been nearly a month since we presented the ballet show for our parents, don't forget," Jenna said.

Heather hadn't forgotten the dance extravaganza. How could she? The *Girls Only* show was one of the absolute best things all year. At least the most creative thing she'd done with her girl friends, including some awesome choreography, blocking, narration, and, of course—the music!

Every other spare minute was spent ice-dancing with her older brother and partner, Kevin. Often they practiced three to four hours a day, four days a week. And every other weekend they spent Saturdays in Colorado Springs, less than an hour away.

"So . . . are you going to tell us about *your* Christmas break, Heather?" asked Livvy. Her auburn hair was pulled back in an emerald green clip that brought out the color of her eyes.

"Kevin and I worked on our compulsory dances," Heather explained. "Business as usual, I guess you could say."

"You two are so-o-o *perfect* on the ice," Livvy cooed. "I've watched you guys skate and, I'm not kidding, you're really good."

Jenna nodded, her black hair brushing her chin. "Livvy's right. You and your brother are a total class act."

"With synchronized steps that are absolutely super," Livvy said, her eyes sparkling. "I don't know how you do it."

Heather forced a smile. "The same way Jenna does her incredible gymnastic routines." She glanced at her petite Korean friend, then back at Livvy. "And the way *you* show your stuff as a free skater."

Opening her spiral notebook, Heather wrote the date in the upper right-hand corner. *Friday afternoon, January 8.* Then, in the center of the page: *Girls Only—Club Minutes.*

"Are we all set to begin?" asked Livvy, leaning her back against the side of Jenna's bed.

"Hold on a minute," said Jenna, wearing a curious frown. "I'm dying to know something."

Livvy giggled. "Uh-oh, watch out."

Heather had no idea what was going on but waited till Jenna scooted closer and began to whisper. "Do you mind if I ask you something personal?"

Shrugging her shoulders, Heather felt awkward all of a sudden. "I . . . guess not. What's up?"

"Well, it's like this." Jenna looked at Livvy and hesitated, turning terribly shy.

"C'mon, spill it," Livvy said, grinning from ear to ear, like she knew exactly what Jenna was thinking.

Jenna took a deep breath, looking right at Heather. "What's it like working so closely . . . you know, with your brother?"

Heather couldn't help herself. She had to laugh. "What do you mean?" she ribbed her friend. But she knew what Jenna was getting at. She was pretty sure, anyway.

"It's just that Kevin's so cute." Instantly, Jenna's olive skin darkened. Livvy, too, looked a bit sunburned.

"So is it safe to say that *both* of you have a huge crush on my brother?" Heather looked first at Jenna, then at Livvy.

"Well, he *is* drop-dead gorgeous," Jenna admitted.

Livvy wasn't quite as bold. "Yeah, he's real . . . uh, fine."

Sighing, Heather understood. Kevin was as handsome as the girls said. Even better, he was a positively awesome Christian—eager to follow God.

"Okay, now back to the question," Jenna insisted.

Heather chuckled. "Do you wanna know what it's *really*

like ice dancing with Kevin?" she repeated.

Livvy and Jenna nodded their heads, eyes wide with anticipation.

"Well, to begin with, my brother's very careful with me on the ice. We practice the hardest moves very slowly at first. He'd feel horrible if he ever dropped me."

Livvy gasped. "Oh yeah . . . I forgot about the lifts and stuff."

"Accidents happen if you're not careful," Heather explained. "I've seen lots of skaters land on their heads and have to get tons of stitches. Even miss a whole season for injuries."

"So it's a dangerous sport?" Jenna said.

"It's like gymnastics or any other sport, I guess. You just have to be careful. But when I'm on the ice, I like to think more about having fun . . . and working hard toward our next medal," Heather said.

She thought back to a practice last week. Kevin and their coach had "walked" her through some new and difficult moves. Because Kevin was taller—and two years older—Heather felt completely safe on the ice with her brother. And he never was bossy or pretended to know more because he was older. Never.

"Kevin and I have been skating together since I was five and he was seven," she told the girls.

"Wow, that long?" Livvy said.

Heather nodded. "I can hardly remember *not* skating with a partner. I guess you could say my brother and I are like two bicycle wheels—where one goes, the other follows."

"I'd be more than happy to be a bike wheel for Kevin Bock," cooed Jenna, her deep brown eyes staring off into space.

Picking up her pen, Heather ignored Jenna's comment and began writing in the club notebook. "So, have we discussed my brother adequately?"

Livvy was giggling, but Jenna pushed her face into the "minutes" notebook. "Hey, what're you writing?" Jenna asked, looking completely aghast.

Playfully, Heather jostled Jenna away and began to read the entry. " 'The very first order of business on Friday, January eighth, was a discussion about Kevin Bock, the secretary/treasurer's thirteen-year-old brother.' "

Jenna and Livvy screeched in unison.

"No . . . no! You can't put *that* in the club notes," Jenna said, eyes wide.

"And why not?" Heather replied, stifling a laugh.

"Because it's just so . . . uncool," answered Jenna.

"Besides, what if an outsider reads the notes?" said Livvy. "What then?"

"Or what if *Kevin* reads them?" Jenna asked, covering her mouth with her hand. "That would be the uncoolest thing!"

Smiling at both of them, Heather closed the notebook. "Okay, then, maybe we should say the talk about my brother was simply off the record."

Jenna and Livvy leaned back against the bed, their eyes rolling around in their heads. Heather knew she'd closed the door on the Kevin thing.

For today, at least.

They went on to discuss other things, but not a word about boys. Instead, they talked about what to do to raise money for their next show—and when it should be. "How about a Spring Dance Festival?" Livvy suggested.

"We could invite Kevin to perform," Jenna piped up, eyes sincere.

Heather shook her head. "Our club is for girls only, in case you forgot."

"Oh . . . for a second, I guess I did." Jenna's face did the weird greenish purple thing again.

"Actually, I could ice dance alone," said Heather. "Just this once." She was surprised how easily she could say those words—*dance alone*—even though it would seem very strange to perform her fancy footwork and moves without her partner. She was thrilled to offer a solo dance because deep inside she had a secret longing. And tonight, she planned to talk to Kevin about it.

If she had enough courage, that is.

CHAPTER 2

Where's Kevin hiding out? Heather wondered.

She scraped the supper dishes and loaded them into the dishwasher. Quickly, she wiped the table clean and shook the place mat over the sink. Then she hurried upstairs to look for her older brother.

Stopping in the hallway outside his bedroom door, she could see Kevin sitting at his desk. Probably doing home-work. When he was off the ice, he usually had his nose in a book.

"Knock, knock," Heather said softly.

"Door's open," Kevin said without turning around.

She smiled. "You probably knew I was standing out here, right?"

"Before you ever said a word." He turned and grinned. "That's what happens when you skate, breathe, and think like your little sister for six years."

She smiled. "Doing geometry?"

"Always."

"Just wondered if you want to take a walk," she said, hoping she could keep up her nerve.

"Now?"

"Sure, why not?" She hoped he wouldn't refuse.

Closing his math book, he got up. "It's dark out . . . and snowy. You sure about this?"

"We could walk down to the Oo-La-La Cafe and get some ice cream," she suggested. "I'm buying."

Kevin's face broke into a wide smile. "Well, if that's the case, we're outta here. Let's see . . . I'll have a double banana split with extra ice cream and triple—"

"Hey, slow down. Who said anything about pigging out?"

"Aw, c'mon." He pretended to sulk, playing along.

"You know what Coach says about eating bad stuff," she reminded him. "Ice cream once in a while, and then only in moderation."

"Hey, it's one thing to get lectured from Coach, but do I have to hear this from my skating *partner*, too?" From his emphasis of the word *partner*, she wondered if he suspected something.

"Better ask Mom and Dad if we can go out," Heather said as they hurried down the stairs. They stopped by the coat closet in the entryway.

"Dad's working with Tommy on his rocket project," Kevin said, reaching for his jacket.

"In the garage?" she asked.

Kevin nodded. "I think Mom and Joanne are out there, too. Last time I checked, they were."

Heather followed him out to the garage, where they found the rest of the family wearing coats and scarves, helping Tommy with his homeschool project. A giant red rocket.

"Is it okay if Heather and I walk down to the mall for some ice cream?" Kevin asked their dad.

"Isn't it kind of late?" Dad said, glancing at his watch. He was a tall, thin man with the same blond hair as Heather and Kevin.

"We'll be home by eight," Heather volunteered.

Dad looked at Mom, who was nodding her head that it was all right. "Okay, but don't be gone long."

"And go easy on the sweets," Mom said as they headed outside. "Remember, you have practice tomorrow."

"Four-thirty comes so early," Heather muttered.

Kevin chuckled. She could see his breath as they walked toward the sidewalk. "You'd think after all these years, getting up before the chickens would be easy," he said.

Heather watched the glow from the streetlights. They dotted the narrow street, three to a block, and the effect against the snow reminded her of their recent trip to Colorado Springs. On the city's West Side, there was an enchanting section of quaint shops and eateries not far from the World Arena—called Old Colorado City.

She wasn't sure why she thought of the place just now as she and Kevin walked in perfect stride. Maybe it was the memory of a ceramic doll in one of the shop windows—a skater dressed in a flowing white dress with silver beads sewn on the bodice, sleeves, and hem. A girl without a partner, soaking up all the limelight. Sharing the applause with no one.

What would that be like? she wondered.

The stillness was awkward and brought her back to Alpine Lake. She sensed that Kevin knew why she wanted to walk with him along the quiet, narrow street on a cold January evening.

Kevin was in tune with her that way. He seemed to know her mood better than most anyone. Even their homeschool friends—and their relatives—said the twosome were as close as twins. If that was actually true, Heather decided there was only one reason for it. All the skating—the lessons, the practicing. Constant togetherness.

For the longest time, she and her brother had been the only two children in the Bock family. Then one day, their parents sat them down and discussed the possibility of adoption. Heather could still hear her father's words, even though she was just a tiny girl at the time. *"A little boy and girl need a home,"* he'd said with glistening blue eyes.

Dad had held Mom's hand as they told of two youngsters orphaned by a fatal car accident. *"Their names are Tommy and Joanne, and they're darling little ones,"* Mom had said excitedly. *"You're going to have a new brother and sister."*

Heather remembered the brightness on her parents' faces. She also remembered the love she felt from them and *for* them. So changing from just the two of them—Heather and Kevin—to the four of them wasn't terribly difficult. For one thing, Mom and Dad were eager to make the transition a smooth one. They worked hard at blending the family;

even gave little Tommy and Joanne skating lessons for several years. Heather remembered how much fun it was to have a new brother—a younger one—and a little sister.

But changing from ice dancing with a partner to free skating by herself would require a lot of dedication and effort. Much more work on her part—a complete regimen of off-ice training, too. After all, Livvy Hudson was one of the best skaters in all of Alpine Lake, and she did many different types of training off the ice. Things like cycling on a stationary bike, lifting small weights several times a week, and skating in the church parking lot on in-line skates. Beside that, she trained with her coach three times a week and practiced on her own every day . . . even on Saturdays!

So Heather knew what was ahead of her. That is, *if* Kevin would agree to let her go it alone. If . . .

"Uh, Kevin," she began when they were within sight of the restaurant. "I need to ask you something."

He sighed, his breath turning to a wispy cloud of ice crystals. "You're not happy with the way we're doing the fish lift?"

She almost laughed. Of course he'd think of something like that. Something related to one of their skating positions. "No," she said softly, "nothing's wrong with the fish lift."

"Are you sure, because if there is . . . we can work on your spiral some more and the preparation and—"

"It's not about that," she said emphatically.

He was quiet for a moment. Then, "What's wrong, Heather?"

Just the way he said it made her feel sick in the pit of her stomach. She was hesitant to tell her brother the truth. Afraid what her new goal—her incredibly exciting ambition—might do to him. So she was silent, too unsure of herself to say what was on her mind.

"Heather?"

"It's nothing to worry about," she said, furious with herself for not having the grit to follow through. She scrambled for something to discuss and remembered that their dad's fortieth birthday was coming up. "We should have an over-the-hill party. Dad would get a kick out of it, don't you think?"

Kevin seemed relieved. "Sure. Let's talk to Tommy and Joanne and see how much each of us want to chip in."

"We get our allowance tomorrow," she said, feeling like an icicle, walking through a daze of mist and snow. And wishing she'd never invited her brother out into the frosty night.

Bottom line: She was a coward, too scared to tell her skating partner the truth. But how could she without hurting him?

This is horrible! What am I going to do? she wondered.

CHAPTER 3

The three of them—Heather, Livvy, and Jenna—were doing their warm-up stretches at the barre on Monday after school. In the far corner of the ballet studio, Natalie Johnston, the dance instructor, was giving the pianist some final instructions.

"Better limber up in a hurry," Heather told her friends as she watched them in the mirror above the barre. "Natalie will be calling us to center stage any minute."

"I still have some kinks in my legs," Jenna complained, shaking her right leg. Then she leaned forward, stretching it again.

Heather nodded, wishing *her* problems consisted of only a few leg kinks and tight tendons. She'd tried again to talk to Kevin before they took the ice during their early-morning practice session. Right before Coach McDonald arrived all fired up about their straight arm lift. He'd called it brilliant—said something about it being positively perfect.

But she'd gotten exactly nowhere with Kevin, partly because he was preoccupied with their dad's fortieth birthday plans. "Mom's all for a big party," he'd said as they laced their skates. "We'll do the black streamers, black everything, over-the-hill party hats—you name it."

Heather had forced a smile and a chuckle, trying to conceal her true colors. Things would be bad enough when she finally came out with it and told Kevin that she didn't want to partner with him anymore. That she wanted to try something brand new.

Livvy was calling, "Hey, Heather. Time to line up."

The opening measures of Beethoven's haunting *Moonlight* Sonata were the cue for center practice—the slow, sustained exercises to improve balance and graceful movement. But for Heather, everything was a big, fat blur. Like a puppet, she followed Miranda Garcia, her tall Hispanic friend—fabulous dancer and Alpine skier. Miranda, too, had high hopes for the Olympics. Someday.

"Hey, Heather. How's it going?" Miranda flashed a big smile.

"Okay," she said, but her thoughts were elsewhere. Sighing, she felt completely frustrated with her lack of heart. She needed to pull herself together enough to talk to Kevin. Had to!

"Something bothering you?" Jenna asked after class.

Heather didn't dare mention her wish to become a free

skater. She couldn't without raising a lot of eyebrows, especially around Jenna and Livvy. They'd never understand—not in a quadrillion years. Mostly because they'd made up their minds (and probably their hearts, too) that Kevin was something extraordinary. A boy to make the heart beat faster, and all that jazz. Which was probably quite true—if you weren't related to him.

For that reason, it would be next to impossible to convince her girl friends that her new mission in life was an excellent choice. For *her*, Heather Elayne Bock. But they would never understand.

She could hear it now. *How can you possibly think of giving up all those years of skating with Kevin?*

And . . .

Are you out of your mind? Your brother's so-o-o adorable. ·

Or . . .

What I'd give for a skating partner like Kevin!

Livvy followed her into the dressing room. "You upset?"

Unsure about what to say, Heather shrugged off the question. "I'm just thinking, that's all."

Livvy's face drooped. "This isn't about our Spring Dance Festival, is it? You're not backing out on us, are you?"

"No, it's nothing like that," she replied, wondering what had caused Livvy to think of their festival plans.

"Then what *is* it? What's got you in a blue funk?" Livvy insisted.

Digging through her sport bag, Heather located her hairbrush and began brushing vigorously, ignoring Livvy.

"C'mon. Something's wrong, Heather. I can see it in your eyes. They're blazing blue."

Heather snorted accidentally. "Sounds like lyrics to a song or something." With that, she walked toward the dressing-room cubicle and pulled the blue curtain across the rod. Grateful for a little privacy, she changed out of her simple practice clothes into jeans and a sweat shirt.

When she opened the curtain again, Livvy and Jenna were staring at her, still wearing their bell-like skirts and tight-fitting pink bodices.

"What's with you two?" she muttered.

Jenna's face sagged. "Maybe we should ask *you* that."

"You're right. . . ." She didn't know what else to say.

"Hey, we're best friends, remember?" Livvy said, sporting her crowd-pleasing smile.

"Yeah, so lighten up." Jenna poked her in the ribs.

Heather wondered how long she could hold out on her friends. "Maybe we oughta have a club meeting," she said at last.

"We just did," Livvy piped up.

"But that was *last* week," Heather said, hoping they'd give it some thought. She just might be able to share her top-secret longing in a secluded setting. Somewhere like Jenna's attic bedroom. The dressing room here at Natalie's ballet studio wasn't the best place for a heart-to-heart talk about her athletic future.

"I think we oughta have a midweek club meeting." This time there was a sense of urgency in her voice. She knew it came through loud and clear because the girls started to nod their heads.

"Sure. We can get together before Friday's regular meeting if you want," Jenna said, glancing at Livvy. "No problem."

Livvy, too, was very agreeable. In fact, she reached out and slipped her arm around Heather's shoulders. "Is this an emergency meeting?" she whispered.

Suddenly, Heather felt like crying. "I . . . I guess you could say that."

"That's all we need to know," Jenna said, taking her place on the other side of Heather. "*Girls Only* club is calling a zero-hour meeting this Wednesday after school."

Livvy looked confused. "What's zero hour?"

"It means, my dear club member, that we've got ourselves a crisis," Jenna answered. "Any time one of us is freaking out, we're gonna alter bylaws and make some changes in the club schedule. And that's all there is to it!"

Heather felt a smile coming. No . . . it was actually a giggle. Jenna Song had a way of making things seem all right.

The threesome walked out of the dressing room and down the hall to the main doors, arm in arm, past Miranda and several other girls. But Heather didn't care anymore. She let the tears drip down her face. All the while, her smile struggled to be strong.

CHAPTER 7

Early the next morning, Heather took a deep breath as she stared at the Alpine Lake mall skating rink. The place looked ten times smaller than she'd remembered since she and Kevin last practiced here. She was definitely spoiled by the beautiful, Olympic-sized rink at the World Arena.

Today, the ice looked exceptionally dazzling and new, like it did right after the Zamboni made its clean sweep. Leaning against the barrier, she waited for her brother to lace up, wondering how to tell him. It wasn't the least bit fair to skate halfheartedly as an intermediate ice dancer. No, it would only be right to tell her brother as soon as possible.

By tomorrow afternoon, she would know precisely what to do. Livvy and Jenna could help her dream up a good way to break the news to Kevin. That is, *after* they got over the initial shock. She sincerely hoped they wouldn't try to talk her out of her new goal. Surely they'd understand.

Why does this have to be so hard? she wondered.

"Straighter, straighter . . . arms must be completely straight for this lift," Coach McDonald instructed. "Careful, now, not too high." He cautioned Kevin not to lift Heather higher than his shoulders. The rule about the height of lifts was a strict one and had to be followed closely.

Still, she enjoyed the feeling of elevation—even if only a few feet off the ice. How exciting it would be to jump high into the air and whirl and spin the way Livvy Hudson did as a novice-level free skater.

Kevin brought her down slowly. He set her gently on the ice, the blade of her right skate making contact with the surface.

"Wonderful, simply wonderful," Coach said, applauding them. "Now, let's do it again."

"Five more times," Heather grumbled.

"What's wrong?" Kevin asked as they skated in unison around the rink.

"Later," she said, wimping out once again.

He reached for her hand as they prepared for the lift. "Ready?" he whispered.

"I'm counting the beats," she said, knowing that she must keep her arms straight for the difficult move.

"One . . . two . . . three!" Kevin reached out, keeping his arms stiff, too, as he lifted her off the ice.

This time the lift was excellent. But they continued to repeat the practice, making their footwork accurately match the meter of the music. Working through the preparation and the actual move with Kevin, she thought back to the first time she'd laced up the boots on her rental ice skates. She was a tiny preschooler, just turned four years old. The feel of the ice beneath her feet was like nothing she'd ever encountered. From that moment on, she knew she wanted to be an ice skater.

Ice-dancing lessons came a year later, after Heather had learned a few skating basics. At that time, she and her brother were so close in size that their parents (and their coach) decided they should train as ice dancers instead of pairs skaters.

At first, neither Kevin nor Heather had understood the difference between pairs skating and ice dancing. So Coach McDonald made an attempt to explain. "In pairs skating, there are side-by-side jumps, spins, and other dangerous moves."

"What kind of dangerous?" little Heather had asked.

"The death-spiral, for one . . . and the hand-to-hand lasso lifts are risky," her coach said.

Back then, Heather had thought pairs skating was much too hard. But she was only five and still tripping on the front porch steps. The idea of skating like a unit of one seemed almost impossible. Especially with her energetic older brother!

"What's ice dancing all about?" was Kevin's question.

"Ice dancing is fancy footwork performed in time with dance rhythms like the cha-cha or the fox-trot. As partners, skaters must demonstrate different styles of music," Coach had told him. "It's like ballroom dancing on ice. And they have to mirror each other, just like in pairs skating."

Later, they learned that there were special holds and positions—all part of the ice-dancing technique. But each partner had to keep at least one skate on the ice at all times. The only exception was allowed during certain lifts and jumps.

After six years of spending many hours each week, perfecting complicated steps and arm positions, Heather was ready to make a change. Maybe the biggest risk of her life!

"Where was your head today?" Kevin asked later as they stepped off the ice. He seemed upset with her, but she had it coming. After all, they were in training for the Summer Ice Spectacular—only six months away. She couldn't fault Kevin for asking.

"You know how it is. Off days and on days . . ." A ridiculous reply, but she wasn't ready to blurt out her plans. Not here at the rink. Not with Coach within earshot.

"No, I really *don't* know, Heather. Maybe you better explain." Frowning now, her brother stood near the barrier and stared. Like he was trying to put things together without a single puzzle piece. "Maybe we should finish that talk we started the other night."

Heather felt trapped. Besides that, Coach McDonald was coming toward them. "Later," she said quickly. "We'll talk some other time."

"So . . . there *was* something on your mind last Friday

night. You bribed me away from my math homework for ice cream, but you didn't finish what you started."

He knew her so well!

She took a deep breath and put on her skate guards. "Well, if you know so much, why don't you tell *me* what I was thinking!"

Kevin shook his head and turned on his heels. He went to sit on one of the wooden benches surrounding the rink. Heather watched him, her heart sinking. They rarely had harsh words between them. Almost immediately, she was sorry about the outburst.

Oh great, she thought. *Now he knows there's something bugging me.*

Yet she didn't know how to smooth things over. They would walk home together, sit across from each other at the dining room table—for homeschool lessons—and eat lunch together, too.

Togetherness was the thing that was beginning to gnaw at her, almost more than anything. She wanted to become something on her own. If only she could break free of the skating partnership. If only she could go it alone!

Coach had a few suggestions for them off the ice, and then they headed for the mall doors. Together. During most of the long walk home, they were silent. They carried their sport bags over their shoulders and tromped down the snowy sidewalk. Occasionally, a brave bird flew overhead, twittering a wintry song.

At the intersection of Main and Cascade Streets, Heather exhaled, letting the arctic air carry her frustration on wings of white frost. Two more blocks to go.

Kevin finally broke the silence. "We were stunning today ... had the same great line and terrific action going on in our feet. Coach thinks we have a good chance at a medal next summer."

Summer Ice Spectacular! What an incredible thrill it would be to take first place. Heather had literally dreamed of the beautiful medal. And it wouldn't be just for her and Kevin to enjoy. They'd share the delight and the honor with their close-knit family.

She could imagine little Joanne wearing it, the medal hanging down to her chubby knees. And Tommy? She knew he'd want to run off with Kevin's and show the neighbor kids on the block.

As for Kevin, he would value the win as much as either of them. After all these years, he was still devoted to working hard. He had perfected his half of their partnership. She was sure *he* had no secret plan to run off and pursue a new skating goal! Kevin was focused on being the best ice-dancing partner ever.

Wishing for an easy solution to her problem, Heather listened as Kevin recounted Coach's approval of their morning workout. She watched his expressive blue eyes and the determination set into his chin. His hair was every bit as blond as hers, cropped short on the sides and fuller on the top. Though a boy, he was almost a reflection of herself— only taller.

Most of all, she knew Kevin's heart. He was a compassionate but highly driven sort of guy. And at thirteen, he seemed to know exactly what he wanted in life. At least when it came to his ice-dancing career. He was headed for Junior Olympics and far beyond. And he was taking his partner with him. Whether she liked it or not!

Unless she jumped off *his* bandwagon and got on board her own, she'd be stuck ice-dancing through her teens and who knows how far into her twenties. She had to change course. As soon as possible!

Groaning silently, she could hardly wait for the *Girls Only* club meeting. By tomorrow afternoon, Livvy and Jenna would have an amazing plan for her to follow.

Surely they would!

CHAPTER 5

"The zero-hour club meeting will come to order," said Jenna, waiting as Heather and Livvy gathered onto her four-poster bed. Sasha, her golden-haired cat, was curled up near the pillows, oblivious to the trio of girls.

"Any old business?" Livvy asked, leaning forward on her elbows. Her stockinged feet waved in the air.

"Let's just get on with it," the president spouted. Jenna's comment made Heather feel nervous. Especially because both Jenna and Livvy were gawking at her, probably eager to hear what was so important. They had every right to know.

Struggling with her feelings, she realized there was only one reason they'd agreed to this special meeting. Only one. It was because of her tears after ballet class. They felt sorry for her.

She studied her friends under the recessed lighting of the newly remodeled attic room. Livvy was as pretty as a picture with deep auburn hair and the greenest eyes ever. Her skating history (awards and competitions) would make anyone proud to say she was her friend. Livvy also loved to write letters, especially the snail-mail kind, because she enjoyed writing in cursive. The feel of a smooth ballpoint pen on fine stationery, she always said, reminded her of ice skating on a perfect ice surface.

Livvy's grandmother had recently moved to Alpine Lake to give her granddaughter "a good dose of mothering." At least, that's the way Livvy described it. Heather knew that Livvy often fought the sorrow in her heart; losing her mother to cancer at such a young age had made Livvy a very private person. Heather and Jenna never pushed for more than Livvy felt comfortable sharing.

Jenna, on the other hand, was as chatty and warm as Livvy was thoughtful and dreamy. An advanced gymnast and ballet dancer, Jen was the only daughter of the village's Korean pastor and his wife. She wore her black hair in a short, perky style, and when she smiled, her dark eyes squeezed shut.

The joy of her life was tiny Jonathan—her newly adopted baby brother. In fact, Jenna was always showing him off to the *Girls Only* club members.

Heather always felt terrific when she visited Jenna, knowing there was a sweet baby just down the hall. Baby Jonathan reminded her of the day her parents had adopted Tommy and Joanne.

"Earth to Heather!" Livvy was waving her hand in Heather's face.

"Oh, sorry," she blubbered.

"You're not sick, are you?" Livvy said, her own face turning a bit pale.

"No . . . I'm fine. It's just that I'm having a tough time these days."

Jenna scooted closer to her. "That's one of the reasons why we have this club, you know. We're your friends, Heather. You can tell us anything."

Anything? Heather wondered about that.

"Maybe we should pray," Livvy suggested.

"Sure, let's," Jenna agreed, touching Heather's arm.

"I *have* been talking to God about things," Heather told them. "But I'm not being selfish or anything. If that's what you think."

Livvy's eyes widened. "About what?"

Taking a deep breath, Heather knew the time had come. It was now or never. "I can't keep this to myself any longer," she said, gazing at one of the dormer windows. The light from the sky gave her courage somehow. "I've decided to quit ice dancing. I want to train with a free-skating coach. Go it alone."

The room was still, except for a little gasp from Jenna. Livvy, however, wore a timid smile, almost as if she was offering encouragement. *She* would know what sort of challenge Heather was up against, switching to figure skating.

"Are you sure about this?" Jenna whispered.

"Definitely," Heather answered, feeling an unexpected surge of confidence. She turned her gaze to Livvy. "Do you think I can make the switch? I mean, do I have what it takes?"

Livvy's face lit up. "I think you'll do super fine."

Heather waited for the question that was sure to come. Jenna was the one to bring it up. "What about your brother? Does Kevin know about this?"

She felt the weight of the world on her. "That's the hardest part," Heather admitted. "I thought maybe you could help me with that. Help me know how to tell him."

Jenna's face was serious. "What can *we* say?"

"Just give me some ideas—how to break it to him," she said, reaching over and petting Jenna's cat.

"Why don't you come right out and tell him?" Jenna suggested.

Livvy didn't seem as sure of that approach. "Maybe it would be better to tell him in phases," she said.

"Like how?"

"You know, uh, bring him to one of my coaching sessions, maybe," Livvy said, her eyes filled with concern. "I'm sure that would get him thinking about what *you're* thinking."

Heather was amazed. "You mean you two aren't gonna try to talk me out of this?"

"Why should we?" Livvy said. "It's your athletic future we're talking here."

"Your choice, too," added Jenna.

Heather was quiet for a moment. "Do you know what I actually thought you guys might say?"

Jenna's dark brown eyes turned curious. "Something

about being out of your mind to abandon your skating partner?"

Heather nodded.

"Well, to tell you the truth, I think you must be," agreed Jenna, putting on a silly smile.

"Yeah, to give up ice dancing with someone so *adorable*?" Heather teased.

Livvy shook her head. "No, seriously, just because a guy is cute—or your brother—doesn't mean you should stick with a partner . . . or your old goal."

"I know. And I'm not."

"But," Livvy added, "you should know that when skating couples split up, they really do mess up their relationship. And usually get off course for a while."

Heather had given that plenty of thought. She hated the idea of setting Kevin back, away from his goals.

"It takes lots of time to develop a solid relationship with a new skating partner," Livvy said.

"Or . . . maybe Kevin will go solo," offered Jenna. "Ever think of that?"

Heather didn't know what to think. For one thing, her idea sounded outright selfish in some ways. And whether Kevin would believe it or not, selfish was the last thing she wanted to be!

"Oh, I wish I didn't have to do this to him," she groaned. "It's gonna hurt so bad."

"Poor Kevin," whispered Jenna.

"No kidding," replied Heather. But she felt much better having shared her dream—and now her dilemma—with

Jenna and Livvy. "You guys are the best."

Livvy grinned and rolled over on the bed. "We know."

"We're the *Girls Only* club," said Jenna. "What do you expect?"

Getting up and stretching her legs at the barre across the long wall, Heather was glad for Jenna's terrific bedroom/ workout room. "Let's practice ballet," she said.

"You're on!" Livvy said, hopping up.

"What's your style?" Jenna hurried to the CD player.

"Something slow and sad," Heather replied. Which was exactly how she felt.

"Something zippy and bright will cheer you up," replied Jenna.

"Probably not," Heather said softly.

CHAPTER 6

First thing Thursday morning, the phone rang. Heather hurried to get it. "Hello?" she answered.

"It's Livvy. Are you awake?"

"Definitely. It's almost time to leave for skating practice."

"I know . . . for me, too," Livvy said. "I was just wondering if you told your brother anything about . . . well, you know."

"Not yet."

"Oh." There was a short pause, then, "I have an idea. Why don't you talk to my coach before you decide anything."

Heather had actually thought of doing that. And she told Livvy so. "It's just that I'm so sure of myself now. Know what I mean?"

Livvy chuckled into the phone. "But it's such a major switch. You've been programmed to be an ice dancer . . .

with a partner. There's a huge difference between that and free skating."

Heather felt hurt. "I guess you just don't understand where I'm coming from."

"Honestly, I'm trying. It's only that you've spent all these years training a certain way—a very *specific* way. Free skating is totally different."

"Please don't try to change my mind, Liv. I need your support, not a lecture." She sighed. "I'm telling my brother right after practice."

"What about your parents?" asked Livvy.

"I'll tell my mom the minute we get back," she replied.

"Oh, Heather, I really hope everything goes super well for you." Livvy's voice was quivering a little.

"Thanks. That means a lot."

"Well, I guess I'll see you at ballet," Livvy said before hanging up.

"Okay, see ya later." She was still holding the receiver in her hand when Kevin came up behind her.

"What's with the phone?" he asked.

Quickly, she hung up, hoping he hadn't heard her end of the conversation. "Just Livvy."

"Ready to go?" asked Kevin, wearing his red-and-blue stocking cap.

She looked up at it and grinned. "You must think it's going to be cold outside."

"I'm prepared," he said, his eyes searching hers, "for anything."

Her heart sank as she headed for the entryway closet.

Reaching for her down jacket, scarf, and warmest gloves, she wondered if she would actually be able to go through with it and tell Kevin.

"Better take a pair of dry socks along," their mother called down from the top of the stairs.

"I always carry an extra pair," Heather replied.

Kevin said he did, too. "We'll be home in time for school at eight-thirty," he said, throwing Mom a kiss.

"From what Coach McDonald says, you two are going to snatch up that first-place medal next summer," Mom said, looking quite radiant in her white terry cloth robe.

"We've got a lot of work to do before then," he said, waving.

It was the way Kevin glanced down at her that made Heather worry.

"Give Daddy a hug for me," Heather said, turning to go.

"Bye, kids. Have a great skate," Mom called softly.

A great skate.

Heather honestly wished it *were* possible for her to change her mind about her goal—about being a free skater. But there was no turning back.

Today was the day!

Thin flakes of snow seemed to hang in the air, teasing the ground. Kevin pointed it out to her, laughing good-naturedly as they walked toward the village mall.

Heather didn't see the humor in it. Nothing was funny

about the snow looking stuck in midair. "There's just no breeze. That's all," she said flatly.

"But it looks like the flakes are standing still," he said, reaching out to touch the snow.

Standing still—stuck—just like my skating future, she thought.

The rest of the way, they talked about one of their cool homeschool projects—a model of a medieval castle. They were constructing it with the help of detailed blueprints, according to historical data, with Tommy and Joanne and several other homeschool families. Actually, Kevin did most of the talking. Heather was trying to muster the nerve to share her new goal with her brother.

"You daydream a lot lately," said Kevin as they headed toward the mall entrance.

"I do?"

"Sure seems like it."

"Well, maybe there's a reason." She paused, wondering what he'd think if she came out with something a little weird. "People who daydream are thinking momentous thoughts."

Kevin opened the door for her. "Life-changing thoughts?"

The question fairly knocked the breath out of her. *Does he know what I'm thinking?* she wondered.

"Well?" he persisted. "Are they . . . life changing?" His eyes were fixed on her, blinking rapidly. Like he was determined to have an answer.

She felt awkward, standing there at the entrance of the

miniature mall. But Kevin wasn't budging. "We better get going," she said at last. "Coach wants us to be prompt."

"Yes, and Olivia Hudson will be showing up soon—for *her* practice session," Kevin said out of the blue.

Heather felt her cheeks grow warm as he turned away. What was he getting at? What did he know?

The area of the mall rink was smaller than the World Arena, by far. But it had a cozy, familiar feel to it. Tall trees were scattered outside the ice rink, strung with little white lights the year round.

Kevin's remark about Livvy made Heather wonder. Maybe he had overheard the one-sided phone conversation, though he would never have eavesdropped purposely. The Bock kids—including Tommy and Joanne—had been taught in their character-building studies that snooping was wrong. She honestly couldn't imagine Kevin standing behind her, or even dawdling around the corner, listening in on her phone call with Livvy. There was just no way!

Yet just now he'd mentioned Livvy Hudson—Alpine Lake's Olympic free-skating hope for the future.

Why?

What *was* he thinking?

The ice was her enemy. Heather fell more times during warm-ups than she ever remembered. She did some high-speed skating on her own, with lots of hard stroking around the rink.

When she and Kevin came together and did two back-to-back run-throughs of their original dance routine, the cha-cha, Heather kept tripping and falling.

Even Coach McDonald seemed concerned. "Must be one of those bad practice days," he muttered, shaking his head as he watched from the sidelines.

"Sorry," she said again and again. But her heart wasn't in it. She just wasn't trying.

"What's happening?" Kevin asked as they continued their warm-up step sequence.

Heather couldn't tell him. Not here, on the ice. Not when they were supposed to be polishing their dance patterns. It would be cruel.

"Are you tired?" he probed.

She felt helpless to answer.

"Should we stop and talk with Coach?"

That would never do. "I'll be all right," she replied, but she knew today's practice was pretty much toast. In her mind, it was their last session together. And she could hardly wait for it to end.

"Have a great skate," Mom had said.

The words stayed with her as she separated from Kevin for some more solo stroking. Coach always had them drill their individual step sequences and turns. So she worked on the bracket—a one-foot turn that often tripped her up. Especially if she wasn't focused. Today was a disaster. She kept at it until Coach turned his full attention to Kevin.

Switching moves, she practiced the rocker—another difficult one-foot turn. The skate blade edge changed at the V-shaped tracing called the cusp, where the skate reversed direction.

All the while, her thoughts were on Kevin. What would her decision do to his Olympic dreams? And what would Mom and Dad say?

She was pretty sure Mom would hit the roof. Well, at first, anyway. But after the notion settled into reality, both Mom and Dad would come around—understand where she was coming from. At least, she hoped so. Heather was counting on their support. She needed them to understand and cheer her on.

In spite of all that, she couldn't seem to give this skating session her best shot. She was finished with ice dancing. Done!

Pretending to be a free skater was the only way to get through the next two hours. So she swirled across the ice, connecting the blades of her skates in clean, silent strokes against the surface.

Kevin's encouraging smile actually defeated her. She wished she had the courage to tell both her brother *and* their coach after practice. That would be the right thing to do.

After what seemed like an eternity, the skating session was over. Kevin was about to put on his skate guards when Heather spoke up. "Can we talk . . . just real quick?"

Coach hovered near, and she heard him take a deep breath. But he nodded to her, as if waiting for an explanation about her lousy performance on the ice. Kevin, on the other hand, was quiet, standing near the railing that circled the rink.

"I've been thinking about something for a long time," she began, hoping this was the right time to say what she'd been planning. "Neither of you will probably understand this. And that's okay."

Kevin's face was terribly sober and his eyes blinked rapidly. "I think I know what you're going to say, Heather," he said suddenly. "And it's all right with me."

She could hardly believe her ears. "You *know*?"

"I've sensed this coming for a while," he told her, glancing quickly at Coach. "Guess we're just too close, huh?"

She didn't know what to say. Kevin's comment was startling, and Coach seemed as baffled as Heather. She hesitated, then blurted the truth. "I want to be a free skater."

Coach McDonald's eyebrows had always been thick, but now they seemed too bushy, nearly hiding his almost stern gray eyes. "No . . . no, I think it would be unwise to try something so different just now, Heather. It would not be in your best interest to change horses in midstream. And certainly not a wise choice, considering your brother's goals."

She figured he'd say something sensible like that. He wouldn't be Coach McDonald if he didn't.

But what puzzled her even more was the way Kevin had stepped back a bit—away from her—studying her now, almost from a distance. He was silent and seemed perfectly content with her decision. This was strangest of all.

"So you don't mind?" she asked Kevin.

A fleeting smile crossed his face. "You're not looking for a debate, are you? You mind's made up, right?"

She was quiet. He knew better than to quiz her this way.

He raked his fingers through his thick hair. "I'll have to look for another partner. That's the end of it, I guess."

She shivered slightly, wondering how her brother could be so confident. Had he already thought this through? Had he heard about her decision from someone?

Not wanting to make a scene—and with Livvy Hudson showing up just then for her lesson—Heather thanked Coach McDonald. "It's definitely been fun. You're a great coach," she said. "I'm sure Mom and Dad will want you to keep working with Kevin."

"And my new partner, don't forget," her brother added.

"Maybe Coach has some ideas about who that might be."

Heather didn't feel the slightest twinge of regret when her coach reached down and gave her a bear hug. "You have no idea what you're up against, young lady. This is not a good athletic move for you. But I'm on your side—keep your chin up, kiddo."

When she stepped back, she noticed the corner of his eyes glistened. "I'm sorry, Coach, I really am. But I have to be honest with myself, don't I?"

He agreed with her, nodding his head up and down slowly. "I can help you with that, if you'll let me."

She couldn't stand here and listen to someone try to talk her out of what she knew she must do. Besides, Livvy Hudson was sitting on the bench within earshot, lacing up.

Kevin was the one to wrap things up. "We'll talk again, Coach . . . later."

"Yes, and I'll be phoning you tomorrow, Kevin," Coach said, his face too solemn.

I have to be honest with myself. . . .

Heather felt numb inside. She knew she'd been the cause. Still, only half of the ordeal was over. Now she had to tell her parents, starting with Mom.

In spite of everything, she felt freer than she had in months. "I was shocked when you said you knew what I was going to say," she told Kevin as they walked home.

He glanced at her. "It's easy to read you. Your eyes give you away."

"Since when?" She didn't like how this conversation was going.

He chuckled. "You should see yourself sometimes. You're a dead giveaway . . . about your feelings."

"I am?"

"Everything shows on your face," he said. "It's there for the world to see."

Well, she certainly didn't like the sound of this! Surely he was just making small talk. He couldn't mean it. Besides, whoever heard of reading someone's face?

"I think you must be getting strange ideas from your sci-fi novels," she lashed out at him.

Their boots *clunking* on the snow-packed sidewalk was the only sound she heard for several paces. Then Kevin said softly, "I won't make this a problem for you with Mom and Dad."

"Thanks."

"I know the sort of girl you are, Heather. You don't change your mind very often. This free-skating thing must be real important to you."

His words warmed her heart, and for a good half a block, she was glad again that he was her brother.

"I'll be doing some serious looking this Saturday when we go to Colorado Springs, though," he said as they turned the corner onto Cascade Avenue—their street. There was eagerness in his voice.

"I know you want to get on with your skating goals," she said as they headed up the front steps to the porch. "And I understand."

Stopping, Kevin turned to face her. "No, I don't think you do," he retorted. "Because if you did, you'd think long and hard about your decision. Bottom line: You just wouldn't do it."

"So . . . you're mad? That's the real truth, isn't it?"

He leaned his hand high against the storm door, looking down at her. "I'll never stoop to anger about this, Heather. God will provide a skating partner for me. You'll see."

"And He'll help me with my free skating, too."

Kevin offered a comforting smile. "Don't worry about telling Mom and Dad. Everything will work out."

Heather patted her brother on the back and went inside. She hoped her former skating partner was right. More than anything.

CHAPTER 8

Kevin's face was everywhere! Even when Heather closed her eyes in the shower and shampooed her hair, she could see the disappointment in his eyes. His jawline had practically sagged as they'd stood on the ice with Coach McDonald after their skating lesson. Now she couldn't get the image out of her mind.

She knew he was hurt. Let him say what he wanted about sensing her intention ahead of time and all that—even sounding so sure of himself about finding another partner. But she knew better. No matter what Kevin had said on the porch this morning, she knew it was her decision that had bruised his ego.

After showering, she dried her hair and went to her bedroom to dress. Mom had always insisted that they wear clean clothes and look presentable even though *their* schoolroom consisted mostly of the dining room table, where they read the Bible together, wrote individual book reports and essays, and worked math problems. The kitchen area was used for science experiments, spreading out historical timelines, and a twice-a-week cooking class. The family room was large enough to build a model Gothic castle and put together an occasional three-dimensional puzzle. Still, Mom was a stickler for neatness. And honesty.

Heather smoothed the wrinkles out of her bedspread and stuffed her dirty clothes in the hamper in the closet. Glancing around the room, her eyes fell on the poster of Jayne Torvill and Christopher Dean, called the greatest ice-dancing team in history so far. The enthusiastic, bright faces of Torvill and Dean had spurred her on many mornings as she dressed for skating lessons or sessions with Kevin on their own.

"I won't be needing this anymore," she said, removing the poster from the wall. Then she carefully pulled off the adhesive from each corner and rolled up the colorful poster. Way in the back of her closet, she stood it on end, out of sight.

The wall looked bare now. Definitely exposed. Just like her dreams and goals had been laid bare to her brother and Coach McDonald this morning. But all of that would have to be worked out.

Sighing, she stared at the empty spot where the poster had been. If her dad's birthday wasn't so close, she might've wanted to spend part of her allowance to purchase something new. A full-length poster of Kristi Yamaguchi—her current inspiration—would be the perfect replacement. Slender and light-footed, Kristi was strong enough to consistently land triple everything. Triple toe loops, triple flips, triple Salchows, and triple Lutzes. Unbelievable!

How many years till I can catch up? she thought of her free-skating dreams. *Am I too late?*

She gathered up her English homework. Along with history, science, and math, her parents were big on grammar. So she and Kevin and their younger brother and sister were reviewing correct sentence structure and usage of verb tenses. They even diagramed long sentences sometimes.

"I want to make sure you know how," Mom would say whenever Tommy whined about it.

Heather didn't mind doing things Mom's way, especially when it came to homeschool. But skating? That was another thing altogether. Would her parents be upset about the money they'd already spent on lessons, ice time, costumes, and everything else?

Nothing's been wasted, Heather reasoned as she headed downstairs for school. She would transfer all her ice-dancing knowledge into free skating. Easy as one ... two ... three.

On the living room bookshelf, she located her Bible and hurried to the dining room. Glancing at her watch, she saw that she was nearly late.

"It's about time," Tommy teased, his brown hair sticking out in the back.

"Did you primp real nice?" Joanne asked, sitting next to Heather at the long table.

"Not much." Heather ruffled her sister's ponytail. "Did you?" She tightened her sister's hair bobble, admiring the shine of the long brunette hair.

Tommy scowled. "Primping's yucky."

"Is not," Joanne said with a frown. "Heather's pretty . . . as pretty as any ice princess who ever lived!"

Quickly, she took her place at the table next to her sister. "What's this about an ice princess?" she asked.

"That's *you* I'm talking about," replied the little girl, offering a grin.

Heather noticed an empty space in Joanne's mouth where a front tooth had been. "Looks like somebody just lost something," she said.

"I sure did," Joanne said, her brown eyes shining.

"Did you save it?" asked Tommy.

Joanne pulled a tiny white tooth out of her pocket. "It's right here. But I'm hiding it from Mommy . . . for a surprise."

"Then you'd better smile with your mouth shut," advised Heather.

Joanne's eyes widened. "How do I do that?"

"Just keep your lips together. Like this." Heather showed her sister how.

"Yeah, but Joanne's got *another* loose tooth," Tommy whispered, pointing to her.

Smooshing her lips together, Joanne let out a peep. "That one's a secret, too."

Overhead, they heard a commotion. It was Kevin, rushing toward the stairs. He flew down them, landing on both feet. "Am I late?" he asked.

"Fifteen seconds!" Tommy hollered, studying his watch.

Kevin pulled out a chair across from Heather. "What's this about a secret?"

"Shh! You mustn't tell," said Joanne and quickly covered her mouth with her hands.

Kevin's forehead wrinkled into a frown. "There are too many secrets in this family."

Tommy and Joanne looked confused. "What're you talking about?" Tommy asked, staring first at Kevin, then Heather.

"Never mind," said Heather. "Mom's coming."

She couldn't help but think Kevin was going to blurt out *her* not-so-secret plan the minute Mom showed up. She even held her breath, but her fears were unfounded. Kevin opened his Bible and seemed to forget.

"Thank the Lord for a beautiful winter day," Mom said, greeting each of them. Fortunately, she didn't inquire about their early-morning skating lesson. Instead, she had them bow their heads and pray about the day's studies.

When their prayers were finished, Mom asked, "Who'd like to read the Bible first?"

Tommy raised his hand. "I will," he said, eyeing Joanne. Her lips were still smashed together, hiding the missing tooth.

"Wait just a minute, Tommy," Mom said, looking at Joanne. "Is something wrong with your mouth, sweetie?"

Heather figured her sister's tooth secret was history. She wondered if now was a good time to bring up her own news. Toying with the idea, she shot a curious look at Kevin. But he was paying no attention to her. His nose was already buried in his Bible.

"My tooth fell out when I bit into my toast," Joanne was explaining to Mom.

"And—gross—she almost swallowed it!" Tommy said, clutching his own neck and pretending to gag.

Mom leaned down and kissed the top of Joanne's head. "Sounds to me like your brother's worried about you, little one."

Kevin must've heard what he thought was a reference to himself. "*Who* am I worried about?" he asked from the opposite end of the table.

Tommy saw his chance and ran with it. "Yeah, you're worried. You said this family has too many secrets. I heard you!"

Slumping down a little, Heather knew what was coming. Her mother was no dummy; she'd taught school for a good number of years before Kevin and Heather were born. Mom knew the tricks kids liked to pull on one another.

"Family secrets, huh?" Mom's big blue eyes were firmly planted on Kevin.

He was nodding, looking a tad bit sheepish. "Better ask Heather about it" was all he said, which was enough to get the ball rolling.

Bible reading and grammar were both put on hold momentarily. And Heather was in the hot seat. Thanks to her big brother. She had no choice but to plow ahead. "I'm quitting ice dancing. I told Coach McDonald today." She stared down at the table. Didn't dare look at her mother.

"Uh-oh," Joanne said.

"Yikes," Tommy whispered.

"What's going on here?" Mom demanded of Kevin. "What's she talking about?"

Heather couldn't believe her ears—Mom was asking her brother instead of her!

"It's true," Kevin answered. "Heather wants to quit ice dancing and be a free skater."

Mom straightened to her full height. "You've got to be joking! Am I dreaming?" Her voice sounded strange. Very weak.

Heather had her chance to speak up. "*I'm* the one dreaming, Mom. It's a fantastic dream, and I really want to do this."

"So . . . you're serious?"

"Definitely. I've never been so sure of anything in my whole life," she said, hoping her mother would understand. "Is it okay with you?"

"Well," said Mom, her face turning slightly pale, "I'll have to think about this." Mom promptly turned and headed into the kitchen.

Heather glanced across the table at Kevin and shrugged. "Now what?"

"She'll come around," Kevin assured her. "Just give her time."

"I hope so." But Heather wasn't so sure. Based on Mom's sickly expression, she decided to get the Bible reading started. Each of them took turns reading until the chapter was finished.

Mom was still in the kitchen when it was time for grammar. Kevin and Heather knew exactly what to do. They assisted their brother and sister with the elementary-level worksheets.

Mom's freaking out, thought Heather. *I'm in big trouble!*

CHAPTER 9

"You and your brother are a perfect match," Mom insisted during a break in social studies.

"I know," Heather said. She couldn't disagree. Everyone who'd ever seen her and Kevin skate together always said the same thing. The truth was they *were* perfect together. But their partnering days were over. "I really want to free-skate, Mom."

"She's just bein' stubborn," Tommy said, waving his chubby finger at Heather.

"Now, Tommy, that's not for you to say," Mom intervened.

Relieved, Heather continued to state her cause. "It's so important to me, Mom. I *have* to try."

Mom shook her head, still frowning. "Is this about the jumps . . . is that what you want?" She was clearly groping for reasonable answers.

Heather wondered how to make her mother understand.

Taking a deep breath, Heather began again. "Yes, it's about jumping, and everything else that goes with free skating. I'll work hard, Mom. I'll do whatever it takes," she promised. Then she looked at Kevin. "I hope my former partner won't take this wrong, but I really want to skate on my own."

At that point, Mom cut off the discussion. She said they couldn't miss any more school time over the debate. Hoping Kevin truly did understand, Heather obeyed her mother and kept quiet about it.

"Girls'll be lining up for Kevin," Livvy told her on the phone that afternoon. "He won't have any trouble finding a new partner."

"Are you sure?" Heather had called to fill her friend in on the day's events.

"There are always girls waiting for skating partners. Especially for super-talented guys like your brother."

"You're right." She paused, thinking about what her next move would be *if* her parents gave permission to take free-skating lessons. "Mind if I watch you work with your coach tomorrow?" she asked hesitantly.

"Sure," Livvy said. "I'll even introduce you to him."

Heather could hardly hold the phone. "You're kidding! That would definitely be cool."

"You'll really like Coach Sterling. I can promise you that," Livvy said.

"Okay, but I'll double-check with my mom first."

"Super. I'll see you first thing in the morning."

"Hope so. Bye, Livvy."

"Hang in there, girl," Livvy said.

Heather hung up the phone. *This is definitely what I want!* she thought and scurried off to the kitchen. There she found Mom cooking supper. The expression on her mother's face was as close to dismal as she'd ever seen.

"I'll help make the salad," she volunteered. "And set the table."

Mom glanced at her, nodding, as though deep in thought. "Thanks, honey."

"I understand if you're upset with me," Heather said softly. "I didn't expect you to be thrilled."

"No, I suppose not." Mom's voice sounded hollow. "But if you're determined—and committed—I'll make a deal with you."

"Really?" She felt breathless. "You'll let me get a new coach and—"

"Listen, Heather. I've already talked to Dad, and he agrees with me on this." Mom paused for a moment, and it was then that Heather saw the hope begin to rise in her mother's eyes. "If it can be worked out with Livvy's coach, I'll pay him to give you one lesson. We'll see how you do with some jumps. Like the axel, maybe."

"You will?"

"I'll give Mr. Sterling a call tonight." Mom turned on the oven light, bending over to peek in at the meat loaf. "But there's a catch to all this," she said, straightening.

"Anything. Whatever you say." Heather meant it.

Mom's eyes were steady, fixed on her. "You must show Coach Sterling—and me—that you won't freeze up on your jumps. That you're not tense or hesitant going into them."

"Is *that* all?" She flung her arms around her mother's waist and squeezed. "Oh, thank you, thank you. I can't wait!"

"Let's see if Coach Sterling has some time this week . . . and if he wants to come out of retirement a little further," Mom said, heading into the dining room.

Heather had to smile because she knew the story behind Livvy and her famous, but retired, skating coach. The older gentleman had come to Alpine Lake to seek refuge from the Lake Placid skating crowd, among other things. He'd agreed to coach Livvy because she was new to the area, having lost her coach after she and her father moved to Colorado. Besides that, Livvy was on track for advanced-level competition. Maybe even the Olympics someday.

While her mother dialed the phone number, Heather went to the window in the breakfast nook. She stared out at the snowy landscape. The side yard between their house and the neighbor's was only a few yards wide, yet with a layer of new snow, the distance seemed more spacious.

Gazing out at the glittery whiteness, she was more than eager to have a lesson with Livvy's coach. But would Coach Sterling agree to give her a single lesson in jumping? If he did—and she could prove to herself *and* to Mom that she had the ability—she would definitely be on her way to a new and exciting career. More thrilling than ice dancing could ever be.

She sighed and sat down at the table. "This is almost too good to be true," she whispered. "But can I pull it off?"

CHAPTER 10

By the time her mother was finished on the phone, Heather had devoured a whole apple, four carrot sticks, and a tall glass of milk.

"Oh, honey, you'll spoil your supper," Mom said, coming into the kitchen.

"Don't worry. I'll eat my share of your meat loaf. I'm starving." She took another bite of carrot, eager to hear about the conversation with Livvy's coach. "Does Mr. Sterling have time to help me?" she asked.

Mom pulled out a chair and sat down. "He's reluctant to commit to another student. Called himself an old man. Mr. Sterling wants to travel more, relax and enjoy life."

Heather's heart sank. "You mean he won't coach me just this once?"

"I don't know, honey. It might not work out," Mom said, her face showing signs of distress. "But on Saturday, when we go to Colorado Springs, I'll check around about a coach for you."

Heather slid down in her chair. "Maybe this isn't such a good idea after all."

"You're not giving up, are you?" Mom said, reaching over to pat Heather's hand.

"Well, no . . . but—"

"But, what? Heather, this may not be an easy situation," Mom reminded her. "If free skating is really what you want, you're going to have to fight for it. Hang in there with me."

Heather sat up straighter. "I know, and I will. It's just that I thought Mr. Sterling might have some time for me." She sighed. "Livvy invited me to watch her skating lesson tomorrow."

Mom smiled. "Livvy sounds like a good friend," she replied. "So many skaters have such a competitive attitude."

Having experienced the gossip and hateful back-biting among other athletes of this sport, Heather knew exactly what Mom meant. "You're right. Livvy's the perfect friend for me."

"So . . . you want to watch her work out with her coach?" asked Mom, a curious smile on her face.

"If it's okay with you."

"Sure, and I'll come along, if you'd like." Mom got up to check the oven.

"Any time." Then she thought of her brother. "What about Kevin? Who'll be his new partner?"

"I asked Livvy's coach about that," Mom said from the stove. "He knows of several skaters in the Colorado Springs area that may be good possibilities."

"That's great," she said. "I'm happy for him." And she meant it.

Definitely.

Heather was getting ready for bed when her little sister came into the room. Joanne closed the door and plopped down on the bed. "I've decided something," she said in her little-girl voice.

"Really? What did you decide?" Heather asked, trying to show some interest.

"I want you to keep my tooth—for the tooth fairy." Joanne handed over a small envelope with the obvious bump. "Here you go."

Heather looked at the envelope. "The tooth fairy might get confused about where to put the money."

"What do you mean?"

"Well, if your tooth is under *my* pillow," Heather said, "won't the tooth fairy get mixed up?"

Joanne paused, wrinkling her forehead into a frown. "I didn't think about that." She sighed. "And Mommy's the tooth fairy, right?"

Heather toyed with telling her sister the truth. "Think what you want."

"What's that supposed to mean?" The smaller girl put her hands on both hips.

"Mom's *not* the tooth fairy, Joanne."

"Then who is?"

Heather waited a moment. "Are you sure you really wanna know?"

"I'm sure."

"Okay, then . . . it's Daddy."

"*He's* our tooth fairy?" Joanne's eyes were round and growing wider by the second. "How can it be Daddy?"

"If you don't believe me, stay awake tonight. And watch with one eye," Heather advised.

"I will! But I'll need this, right?" Joanne snatched up her little envelope with the tiny tooth inside.

Closing her door behind her, Heather leaned against it. She thought back to when she was six years old—her little sister's present age. Back then, had she wanted to be a figure skater, doing fancy jumps and spins all over the ice? She tried to remember. For all her skating career, Kevin had been at her side. She'd never skated alone on the ice, except for solo stroking and working out her part of their dance programs.

"Tomorrow's just the beginning," she whispered, glancing at the empty spot on her bedroom wall. Ice dancers Torvill and Dean were gone now. It was time for a free skater to take their place. Tomorrow, after school, she'd go to the mall and buy a new poster.

Slowly, she walked to her dresser and picked up her hair brush. She began her nightly routine. Twenty-five times on each side. Mom said vigorous brushing made her hair shine under the spotlights on the ice.

She thought of seeing Livvy tomorrow—and meeting

her coach. She'd seen the old gentleman enough times to know who he was but had never been formally introduced.

Everything Livvy had told her about Odell Sterling was amazing. The man had coached many talented and dedicated skaters—including three World Champions. Two of his students had placed high at the Olympics and were now instructors themselves.

"If I could just get Mr. Sterling to help *me*," she said to the earnest face in the mirror. "Maybe then I'll have a chance. . . ."

Before she read her Bible and devotional book, Heather crept out of her room and down the hall. She knocked on the door of her parents' bedroom. Mom appeared, dressed in her white bathrobe. "Can you tell you-know-who that Joanne has a baby tooth under her pillow?" she whispered.

Mom grinned and hugged her good-night. "I'll tell Dad about it. Thanks, Heather. I completely forgot."

Tiptoeing back to her room, Heather wondered about her mother's remark. It was unlike Mom to forget important stuff. Heather hoped her plan to skate solo wasn't going to cause problems at home.

Before she fell into bed, she prayed. "Dear Lord, if I'm supposed to be a free skater, will you work things out for me? And since the whole family's affected by my decision, well . . . help all of us." She paused. "And, please, will you help Kevin find the perfect partner to replace me? Thanks for everything. Amen."

The light from her windows was soft and white. She was sure the moon must be full. But when she sat up in bed and looked for it, she saw only twinkling stars. High in the heavens.

It was at night that she always felt closest to God. She didn't know why. She just did.

CHAPTER 11

"Today's the day," Heather announced at breakfast, thinking of Livvy Hudson's invitation to watch her skating lesson.

"And it's *my* day, too!" Joanne showed off two quarters. "The tooth fairy found my tooth and gave me some money. Now I'm rich!"

Heather laughed as she observed the knowing exchange between her parents. "See, I told you to put your tooth under your own pillow," she said, pouring orange juice.

Joanne tilted her head, studying her father. "Are you really the one who left the quarters?"

Dad leaned back in his chair and inhaled slowly. "Well, now, are you sure you want to know?"

"Oh, Daddy, I *know* it was you," Joanne squealed. "I saw you!"

Dad was chuckling now. "You must've been dreaming, kiddo."

Joanne slid back her chair and ran to the head of the table. "You're the tooth fairy! Heather said so!"

Reaching down, Dad squeezed Joanne and gave her a kiss on the forehead. "Well, I guess I've been caught," he said, looking over at Mom. "Looks like our secret's out."

Mom folded her hands, her face bright. "It was fun while it lasted."

"Can't we still hide our teeth when they fall out?" Tommy pleaded. "Even if Joanne knows who the tooth fairy really is?"

"What do you think, Mommy?" Dad asked, wearing a mischievous smile.

Mom shrugged and nodded. "It's okay with me." Her response brought cheers from Tommy and Joanne.

Heather gave Kevin a sidelong look. He was smiling at their younger brother and sister. "Well, I'm glad that important issue's settled," teased Kevin.

When they bowed their heads, Dad began their short-sentence family prayer. Joanne was last because she was the youngest. "Thank you, God, for making my tooth come out with no pulling," she said. "And give Kevin a nice skating partner real soon."

After the prayer, Heather watched her older brother drink his juice. She picked up her spoon to eat the whole-grain, sugarless granola, homemade by Mom. "What qualities are you looking for in a partner?" she asked, almost shyly.

Tommy spoke up. "Has to be a girl, right?"

"Of course," said Heather, cracking up. Mom and Dad were laughing, too.

Joanne had an opinion. "Get someone real pretty. I think that's real important."

Mom sighed audibly. "How about just someone who skates well, has a good attitude, and is committed to hard work?"

Kevin was nodding now and smiling across the table at Heather. "A Christian partner would be nice."

Tommy looked over at Heather. "Are you really sure you wanna quit skating with my brother?" he asked, wrinkling his nose.

Kevin leaned back against his chair the way their dad often did. "To tell you the truth, Tommy, I hope to find someone just like Heather."

Feeling a surge of sudden embarrassment, Heather ate silently. Was Kevin saying that to make her feel guilty? Yet, knowing her older brother as she did, she was pretty sure he was just being nice. Nothing more.

"She's real special, our Heather." Dad winked at her when she looked up. Mom, on the other hand, didn't say a word. But her happy face spoke volumes.

"Thanks, Dad, but you really don't have to say that," Heather said. Then, turning to Kevin, she added, "And neither do you."

"I know, but I mean it," her former skating partner admitted.

She didn't quite know how to take his remark. Was he trying to get her to change her mind?

At the mall rink, there were eight other skaters besides Livvy on the ice when Heather and her mom arrived. Some were stroking around the rink for fun. Others were practicing spins and easy jumps.

And there was Kevin, going through his dance routine, then doing some hard stroking. Alone.

"Heather, over here!" called Livvy, motioning to them.

"C'mon," Heather said, pulling Mom along.

Livvy's coach was leaning on the rail circling the small rink. He wore a pair of gray dress slacks and a maroon-and-gray patterned sweater. Dashing as usual. He nodded politely when Heather and her mother approached.

In a flash, Livvy skated over to them. "Hey, Heather," she said. "Hello, Mrs. Bock. Heather said you might come along. It's nice to see you."

"Nice to see you, too," said Mom.

Livvy's coach perked up his ears. "So this must be Heather Bock, the girl I've heard so much about," he said, eyes beaming.

"Yes, this is one of my best friends, Heather, and her mother, Mrs. Bock," Livvy said, introducing them.

Mr. Sterling extended his hand to each of them. "Delighted, I'm sure." Had he been wearing a hat, Heather was almost positive the man would have tipped it politely.

They sat down and watched Livvy run through her programs without a single break in between. She was obviously in good shape, Heather thought. And when Livvy did her jumps, Heather wished she were out on the ice with her, learning what to do.

"Let's see the double Lutz again," Mr. Sterling called to Livvy. His voice was calm and matter-of-fact. Not demanding like some coaches Heather had observed.

She watched as her friend worked up the momentum to do the jump. First came the long, powerful glide to set it up. Then, using the toe pick on her free foot, Livvy took off from the back, outside edge of her skating foot. Up . . . up she flew.

Heather held her breath as Livvy made two complete rotations and landed on the back, outside edge of her free foot.

"Perfect!" Heather said from the sidelines, recalling every aspect of the jump—the setup, the lift into the air, the revolutions, and the beautiful, clean landing.

"I can do that," she told her mom. "I just know it!"

Mom squeezed her hand and watched the rest of the session.

When Livvy's time was up, Mr. Sterling came over again. "You're welcome to stop by and visit anytime," he said.

"Thank you," Mom said, getting up. She was probably headed down to talk to Kevin, who was working out alone on the ice.

"Mr. Sterling, can you *please* teach me how to jump?" Heather asked. She surprised herself with her boldness.

Mom looked aghast. "Heather, I already discussed this with Mr. Sterling." Her words were pinched like she was talking through her teeth.

The old man's face seemed to light up. "Yes . . . yes, as a

matter of fact, we *did* speak of a jump lesson, didn't we, Mrs. Bock?"

Heather's heart skipped a beat. "I'll work really hard, and I won't take up much of your time." She was pleading now, but she couldn't help it.

Livvy was standing behind her coach, nodding to Heather. She was grinning from ear to ear. Heather took that to mean she should keep it up, but her mom was actually glaring. "We don't want to impose on you, sir. You'll have to excuse my daughter's eagerness."

Worried that her mother's comments might hinder things, she began to pray silently. She hoped so hard she thought she might burst.

Mr. Sterling turned around, nearly bumping into Livvy. "You say Heather is your friend?"

"Yes, and she's one super cool skater," Livvy said, her hair bouncing against her face as she nodded.

"In that case, I'll see what I can do," the man replied.

Heather hugged her mom and Livvy both. And if Mr. Sterling hadn't stepped back a bit, she might've hugged him, too. "This is the most awesome day of my life," she said.

Mr. Sterling's cheeks turned an embarrassed pink. "Meet me here next Monday morning." He looked at his watch. "At say, eight-twenty. We'll have a jump lesson, Miss Heather— you and I."

"Oh, Mr. Sterling, thank you very much," she replied. "I'll be here, right on time."

"You're *very* welcome," Mr. Sterling said with a nod.

Then he added, "I must say I do admire persistence."

Heather and her mom turned to go.

"Good-bye, Mrs. Bock," Livvy called.

"You're a wonderful skater," replied Heather's mother. "Keep up the good work."

"Bye, Heather," Livvy called. "See you at Jenna's this afternoon for our regular club meeting."

She waved at both of them—Livvy *and* her coach. And she could hardly wait till Monday morning!

CHAPTER 12

A ballot box—fashioned in tin foil—was balanced on the barre when Heather arrived. The *Girls Only* club meeting was about to begin.

"Off the record, I have some exciting news," Heather said, settling down on the floor.

"Yes, and it's super cool news, too," said Livvy.

"Well, let's hear it," insisted Jenna. She was holding her cat in her lap. Sasha opened both eyes, blinked twice, then gave in to dreamland.

"Livvy's coach is going to give me a jump lesson!" Heather announced.

"Cool stuff," Jenna said, offering a high five. "What's next after the first lesson?"

Heather explained her mom's deal. "If I can actually jump, then Mom'll look for a coach for me."

"Maybe Coach Sterling will take you on," Livvy said.

"I won't move in on your territory," Heather assured her.

Livvy shrugged. "Coach Sterling doesn't belong to me."

The girls continued their bantering, talking about Jenna's "horrid" science project and Livvy's friend Mrs. Newton, the cheerleading coach.

Heather described her five-page handwritten report on Israel ... *and* her little sister's tooth. "Joanne found out today that our dad's the tooth fairy," she said.

Jenna's eyes were big. "That's just cooler than cool. I mean, most dads aren't really all that involved in the fun stuff."

"Well, my dad is," Heather replied, feeling proud to say it. And it was true, too. Her father made it a point to hang out with all four of the Bock kids, taking them skiing in the winter, swimming near Twin Lakes in the summer, backpacking at Breckenridge in the autumn, and, of course, attending all the skating events throughout the year.

She wondered how much more hectic her parents' lives would be with Kevin and his new skating partner competing at all sorts of different times than Heather's solo performances. Her whole family would be busier than ever—running in all different directions, too!

"I think it's time we call our meeting to order," Jenna said, lifting Sasha off her lap. She got up and went to the barre, carrying the foil-wrapped ballot box.

"What's that for?" Heather asked, noticing the red heart stickers on the box.

Jenna set it down in the middle of the circle. Smiling, she raised her eyebrows. "As president of the *Girls Only* club, I'd like to propose that we expand our membership."

Livvy looked surprised. "By how many?"

"Four's a nice, even number," Jenna explained. "If we had four girls, we could practice ballet better. Maybe even double up on some dance projects."

"Partners, like in kindergarten?" Livvy teased.

Heather listened carefully, wondering why a threesome wasn't an okay number for their club.

"So . . . what does the vice-prez and the secretary/treasurer think?" Jenna asked, sitting on the floor.

"Are we gonna campaign for members or what?" Livvy asked.

Heather stared at the Olympic Rings flag mounted high on the wall above the computer desk. "All three of us have athletic goals. If we added another member, she'd have to be a sports nut, too," she said at last. "Just like us."

"Yep," Jenna agreed. "That's the most important part of our bylaws."

Opening the "minutes" notebook, Heather found the rules for club membership. They'd written them on the first meeting, months ago. "Okay, here we go. 'The president, vice-president, and secretary/treasurer agree to encourage each other's athletic aspirations. We will uphold the goals and dreams of each of our members.' "

"It doesn't say a word about adding new members," Livvy pointed out. "But I think it's a super good idea. What do *you* think, Heather?"

"Shouldn't we just vote on it?" she replied, feeling pressured.

Jenna nodded. "I motion that we vote to add another

member to the *Girls Only* club. The coolest cool club ever!"

"I second it," said Livvy.

"Uh, before we do anything," Heather spoke up, "are we voting on four members total?"

"Could be," Jenna said, fidgeting. "Maybe more."

Livvy looked at Heather. "How do you feel about four?"

She felt funny being put on the spot. "I thought we were voting, *secret* ballot," she replied.

"Hold everything." Jenna scurried to her desk for some paper to make ballots.

"I think the prez has someone in mind," whispered Livvy.

Heather wondered who it might be. "Why don't we just talk about the new member instead of voting about how many?" she suggested when Jenna sat back in the circle.

The prez gave each of them a ballot and a pencil. "First things first," said Jenna. "Like the bylaws say."

Heather knew the bylaws weren't etched in stone. She'd read through the bylaws enough times to memorize them. There was nothing in there about additional members. "When we started this club, we never said anything about more than three members. What's wrong with just us?" she asked.

"Nothing," Jenna insisted.

"But maybe Jenna's idea is something to think about," Livvy added quickly.

They discussed the notion of four members instead of three. Then they voted. One by one, they stuffed their folded ballots into the big box.

"Drum roll!" Jenna shouted, turning the box over and fishing out the ballots. She turned her back and counted the ballots. "Two against one—two yesses and one no," she said in nothing flat.

Everyone knew, of course, who'd voted "no." And Heather definitely felt weird about it.

"Majority wins," Jenna announced, throwing away the ballots.

"The secretary/treasurer is supposed to count those, right?" Heather said, upset at Jenna's take-charge manner.

"What's it matter?" said the prez.

"It's in our bylaws who counts the ballots," explained Heather.

"Well, if it's in the bylaws, I guess we just messed up." Jenna marched across the room to the trash can and emptied it onto the floor.

"Jenna, *please* don't do this," Heather said. "Put the ballots back in the trash. It's okay."

"The secretary/treasurer must count the ballots," parroted Jenna.

"Don't be ridiculous," Heather replied, glancing at Livvy, who'd buried her head in two pink pillows.

Jenna sneered, "Well, if you think *I'm* ridiculous, what about someone who changes her skating goals in the middle of her career. That's ridiculous, Heather Bock, and you know it!"

"Excuse me?" Heather was horrified.

"You wanna dump your partner and go for broke," Jenna said. "That's real stupid, if you ask me!"

Livvy's head was still hidden. She was staying out of it.

"Who said anything about dumping my partner?" Heather retorted.

"Well, that's exactly what you did!" Jenna's eyes bored into Heather.

"Look, I'm not gonna argue with you. What I did is between Kevin and me. He's cool with it, and so am I."

Jenna was quiet for a moment. Then she shoved the ballot box across the room, where it came to rest under her desk.

Livvy slowly emerged from the pillows. "Uh, excuse me . . . may I say something?"

Jenna glared. "Whatever."

Livvy seemed hesitant to continue and started to cover her head again.

"Go ahead, Liv," encouraged Heather. She hoped maybe Livvy would talk some sense into the prez.

"I'm thinking that . . . well, maybe this thing about adding members oughta wait," Livvy said softly. "Let's make sure we can get along—just the three of us—before we add someone new."

"I'm with Liv," said Heather.

Livvy was tactful and kind. "We're a club of girls who care about each other, right?" She didn't wait for an answer. "We shouldn't have to argue to solve our problems."

Jenna was nodding her head. "We voted and the vote stands. Now I have a recommendation."

Heather wished she'd stayed home. Better yet, maybe someone else could take her place in this horrible club!

Jenna stroked her cat while she continued. "Miranda Garcia might be an excellent choice for our club," she said. "She's a fabulous downhill skier and ballet dancer. A Christian, too."

They already knew this info about Miranda. What was the big deal? Heather wondered. "So why not invite *all* our church girl friends who have Olympic dreams?" she said.

Jenna nodded. "Fine with me," she said. "What do you think, Livvy?"

"Personally, I like the idea of a small club. Don't forget, I'm an only child—not so used to lots of sisters."

Jenna seemed to understand. "Up until last year, I was the only kid in my family, too. I guess you might be right. Heather too."

Sighing, Heather was starting to feel better about this discussion. "Miranda *is* a good choice," she agreed. "Let's vote on including her."

Jenna began cutting more ballots. "I'm sorry, Heather, about what I said before. I shouldn't have gone off like that. Forgive me?"

Heather nodded. "I guess I just wasn't ready to change things in our club. It's real comfortable, like having two sisters my own age. Definitely cool."

Jenna and Livvy came over and hugged her. "Change is tough," Livvy said. "I should know."

Heather was pretty sure Liv wouldn't explain. Her mom's death and their recent move from Illinois had been difficult for Livvy and her father.

After more talk about the club, they voted on their mutual friend Miranda Garcia. "Does Miranda know about *Girls Only*?" asked Livvy.

"I've kept the club top-secret," said Jenna.

"Me too," said Heather.

"Maybe Miranda won't wanna join," Livvy said, laughing.

Jenna's face broke into a broad smile. "I have a feeling she'll like the club. It's just her and her mom at home."

"Super good thinking," Livvy said.

"Who should invite Miranda to join?" Jenna asked.

Heather volunteered. "I will."

Jenna was all smiles. "Cool. The meeting's adjourned," she said. "Who wants to see my baby brother?"

Heather and Livvy both followed Jenna down the hall to the nursery. The room was aglow in sunlight, and Jonathan was just waking up.

"Oh, he's so sweet," cooed Heather, touching his tiny yellow bootie.

"He has undeveloped gymnastic ability," Jenna informed the girls. "Watch his left foot."

Sure enough! Heather noticed a jerking, forward motion. He nearly kicked off his little bootie. "I think you're right."

Just then Jenna's mother came smiling into the room. "Is my little fella ready for his supper?" she asked, reaching down to pick up the round bundle.

"Better hurry. He's not howling yet," Jenna said.

The girls followed Mrs. Song downstairs and watched her give the baby his bottle.

Jenna served up a lemon-lime concoction she made in a

blender, complete with crushed ice. "To our health!" she said, holding her glass high.

"To our Olympic futures!" Livvy added, doing the same.

"To our new club member!" said Heather, joining in.

CHAPTER 13

When Heather was limber enough, she stepped onto the ice at the World Arena Ice Hall. Kevin had come to look for prospective skating partners. Mom too.

Heather would simply enjoy the ice time, practicing old moves and a few easy spins. For fun. The mall rink in Alpine Lake seemed to be shrinking by the day. An hour stint on the Olympic-sized rink was definitely a nice change.

"What do you think of the skater with the jazzy purple outfit?" Kevin asked, catching up with Heather.

"Where?"

"The blond girl . . . over there." He pointed to a young skater halfway across the rink. "What do you think of her skating?"

Heather spotted the girl. She was short and squatty—all hips. But her purple practice pants were eye-catching. "I'll let you know in a minute," she told him.

"Promise?"

"Of course I promise," she said. Her brother was acting so weird today. Demanding and pushy. In fact, all he'd wanted to talk about on the trip down was a skating replacement.

While she stroked around the rink, Heather kept her eye on Miss Purple. The girl was a so-so skater, in Heather's opinion. She knew she'd have to be careful what she said to her brother. Kevin would think she was being picky. Actually, she was trying to be as objective as she could about Kevin's choice.

Meanwhile, Mom was busy chatting with several coaches. Heather glanced her way every so often, wondering if her very particular mother might be lining up interviews for next week. Of course, Heather knew she'd have to convince Mom that she could actually pull off the jumps and spins required to be a free skater.

"So . . . what's the verdict?" Kevin was back. He'd snuck up behind her while she was watching Mom in the stands.

"To be honest with you, I think you can probably find someone better than Miss Purple."

"Okay, then, what about the pink number over there?" Kevin said, a twinkle in his eye.

The skater in pink was perky and cute—about Heather's build and height. She had long, graceful lines and the shiniest, bounciest brown hair Heather had ever seen. And she could do flying spins like nobody's business!

Kevin stayed close to Heather as they moved around the rink. Occasionally, he touched her elbow or waist the way he often did during their dance routines. Heather found it both annoying and amusing, thinking it was most likely second nature to him.

"Wow, she's really good," she heard him say.

"Better introduce yourself quick," Heather suggested, "before she gets away."

"Come with me, okay?" Kevin asked, looking unusually shy.

"No . . . you go by yourself," she insisted. "This isn't my thing anymore." With that, she sped up, gliding across the rink.

"Heather, come back!"

Deep in her heart, she felt a stabbing pain. Never before in all her life had she turned her back on Kevin this way. She had done it twice, really. Once when she'd quit dancing with him and now today, when he'd asked for her input.

What's wrong with me? she thought. *What's happening to us?*

Then she remembered what Livvy had said about skating couples who split up. *"They mess up their relationship,"* Livvy had said. *"And sometimes set their careers off course."*

But Heather didn't think she had to worry about spoiling their relationship. After all, she and Kevin were brother and sister. Nothing too terrible was going to happen. They lived in the same house, shared the same parents and the same younger brother and sister. She was sure things would be just fine.

Watching from afar, Heather found herself holding her breath. Kevin skated up to the girl in pink, and the skater burst into a big smile. Kevin was smiling, too.

Before long, he began skating with the girl. They talked and laughed, stroking leisurely around the rink. At one point they stopped, and he showed her a step sequence. The skater watched carefully, then imitated Kevin's footwork almost perfectly.

Girls will be lining up to skate with Kevin. . . .

The twosome skated around the rink two more times. But when they stopped to talk to her mother, Heather knew Kevin must be thinking seriously about auditioning the girl. Had he found his new partner?

"Cynthia's strong and very athletic, don't you think, Mom?" Kevin babbled all the way home.

"We'll see how the two of you work together" came Mom's answer.

"But she's so expressive," Kevin continued.

Mom nodded. "Yes, I noticed that. But she's never had a partner before. That will take some getting used to."

"So when can we start?" he asked, obviously eager.

"Let's discuss it with Dad," Mom replied. "He'll want to meet Cynthia. So will Coach McDonald."

Kevin grinned. "Fair enough."

Heather was sure her brother had his heart set on the brunette skater. "She might be a good choice" was all she said.

"Might be?" Kevin replied, looking wounded. "Cynthia's my age, for pete's sake!"

Leaning against the window, Heather thought about her brother's reaction to the prospective partner. She wondered if he was really all that excited about ice dancing with her. Maybe he was, but she suspected there was more to it. Kevin had all the signs of a major crush on Cynthia Whoever.

Best of all, though, Heather was soon to be off the hook. Ice dancing with Kevin was completely over. Now, if she could just make it till Monday morning and impress the socks off Livvy's coach. And Mom!

CHAPTER 14

Sunday after church Heather phoned Miranda Garcia. "How's it going?" she asked, making small talk.

"Busy. You know how it is with ballet and school and stuff."

"Do you have any extra time to, like, join a club?" she asked right off.

"What sort of club?"

"It's called *Girls Only*. So far there are three of us," she explained. "Jenna Song, Livvy Hudson, and me."

"Really?" Miranda seemed interested. "What do you do?"

"Last month we presented a Christmas show for our families. Right now we're working on a dance festival for spring. We like to practice ballet moves and, you know, hang out at Jenna's house—that's where we meet."

"I heard she has a barre and a huge wall mirror in her bedroom," Miranda remarked.

"That's true. Jenna's bedroom is in the attic. There's lots

of room for all of us to practice at the barre."

"Good, then, count me in."

"We're mostly about athletic goals and Olympic dreams," she went on to say. "I think you'll get a better feel for it when you come."

"When's the next meeting?" asked Miranda.

"We get together on Fridays, right after school. And we always eat healthy snacks, so don't worry about junk food or sweets."

"Great. Thanks for inviting me," Miranda said.

"Uh, you might wanna keep it a secret because so far it's just the three of us—with you, four. But we'd rather not get too big, you know what I mean."

"Sure do. Thanks, Heather. See you at ballet."

"Okay. Bye."

Heather hung up the phone. *That was easy*, she thought and hurried downstairs.

She found Kevin whispering in the kitchen with Tommy and Joanne. He turned around quickly, like he'd been caught red-handed. "Oh, it's you. That's okay," he said.

"What's up?" she asked, opening the fridge.

"Keep your voice down," Tommy bossed.

Joanne was gesturing for her to come over. "We're talking about the tooth fairy's birthday," she said. "He's turning the big four-oh."

Kevin smiled. "We're pooling our allowance," he explained for Heather's sake.

"To get something really special for Daddy," Joanne whispered.

"Does Mom know?" asked Heather, glancing over her shoulder.

"It's just our secret," Tommy said. "And you have to promise not to tell."

Heather laughed. "Oh, I'm good at keeping secrets. Trust me."

The phone rang, and Kevin ran to get it. Heather stayed with Tommy and Joanne because she was certain the call was for Kevin. Probably from Cynthia, the skater they'd met yesterday.

"That's Kevin's girlfriend, right?" Tommy asked.

"Beats me," she said.

"Kevin acts real silly all the time," Joanne piped up.

Heather agreed but kept her thoughts to herself.

When Kevin came back, he looked mighty happy. "That was Cynthia. She's coming to Alpine Lake tomorrow afternoon to meet with Coach McDonald."

"Really, that soon?" Heather tried not to show her surprise.

"Yep. Everything seems to be working out." Kevin opened the cupboard and pulled out some beef jerky. He pulled it apart, dividing it into four pieces. "Who wants to share this?"

Tommy and Joanne did, of course. Heather refused.

The kids decided how much money the four of them had between them. All totaled: twenty dollars. Enough to buy a brand-name tie for their dad.

"A really *special* tie," Joanne insisted.

Before church that evening, Heather went upstairs to

her room and rested. She fell asleep, dreaming that she was skating alone under a starlit sky. One of the stars seemed so bright, she just assumed it was a spotlight. But when she looked again, she saw that it was the moon.

Livvy Hudson was at church that evening. She seemed delighted when Heather invited her to sit with them. "We're one big, happy family," Livvy said, sliding in next to Kevin.

"Better watch it," Heather warned. "My brother's got a girlfriend."

"Who?" whispered Livvy.

"Tell you later." And she did. Right after the benediction, Kevin got up and filed out of the church. But Heather and Livvy stayed in the sanctuary for a few minutes longer.

Quickly, Heather filled Livvy in on the latest. "Her name is Cynthia Something, and she's coming to meet Coach McDonald. Tomorrow!"

"Aw, phooey," Livvy said, eyes downcast. "I was hoping he'd pick *me* for his skating partner."

"You?"

"Sure! I'd love to skate with someone like Kevin."

Heather could hardly believe her ears. "You're the best free skater around here. What're you talking about?"

"Gotcha," Livvy said, wearing an ear-to-ear grin. "I think you'd better relax about this."

"I'm trying. I really am."

"Could've fooled me," Livvy said as they walked toward

the church foyer. "See ya tomorrow, bright and early?"

"You're coming?"

Livvy gave her a hug. "I wouldn't miss it for anything."

"Thanks." Heather went home and counted the hours, minutes, and seconds till her appointment with Livvy's coach. But when she prayed, she told God she was definitely nervous. "But you'll be there to help me, right, Lord?"

The moon was nowhere to be seen as she slipped into bed. The light from the back porch spilled out far past their snowy yard. The night was bright enough.

So was her future.

CHAPTER 15

Heather and her mom arrived at the mall rink ten minutes early. She laced up the boots of her skates, keeping the skate guards on. Leaning on the rail, she watched a skater at the far end of the ice.

The girl skated across the ice toward Heather. With a solid, upward motion she brought her right leg up and forward, then shot into the air. Her legs flew apart into a wide, clean split high above the ice. Then she landed on one skate, dipping down to a sit spin position. Spinning around in a blur, she came to a stop with her hands raised overhead.

"Wow," whispered Heather. "That's exactly what I want to do someday."

"You'll have to work very hard," Mom said, offering an encouraging hug.

"I know, and I'm ready for it." She looked at her watch. "Coach Sterling's late."

"Here he comes now," Mom said, looking over her shoulder. "And Livvy's right behind him."

Heather felt herself relax a bit. She knew she was psyched for this moment—had even worried that something might happen to prevent or delay the jump lesson. But seeing Livvy and her famous coach, Heather breathed a deep, confident breath.

She circled the rink several times to get the feel of the ice beneath her skates. *A single loop jump—an edge jump*, she thought. Livvy's coach had picked the easiest jump of all.

Concentrating on her feet, Heather took a deep breath. She enjoyed the feeling of freedom. No one holding her hands or waist. She could move at will. On her own!

She was ready to try the jump. Off from the back, outside edge of her skating foot, she lifted herself up. One rotation—to form the look of a loop in midair—and down. She landed on the back, outside edge of her takeoff foot.

"Excellent!" Coach Sterling called to her.

The loop jump was too easy. She should try something harder this time. And Livvy's coach didn't disappoint her. "Let's have you attempt the flip jump next," he said, motioning to her.

Listening carefully as Mr. Sterling described the jump, Heather remembered how the jump looked when Kristi Yamaguchi or even Livvy Hudson performed it. Same as the Lutz, but it took off from the back, inside edge of the skating foot—not the outside edge. And it was a toe pick–assisted jump.

When it was time, she stroked hard to build up speed. Then, turning backward, she glided across the ice. She used her toe pick to help her spring into the jump. But she fell on the landing. "I'll try it again," she said, getting up.

This time she landed on the wrong foot. But she wasn't one to give up easily. She tried again—four times more. By the fifth try, she landed on the back, outside edge of her free foot.

"Yes!" Livvy shouted, clapping on the sidelines. "You did it!"

The flip jump hadn't been perfect, but Heather was excited. And by the end of the hour, she'd landed two more single flips and was trying for the next hardest—the Lutz.

"You're super incredible!" Livvy said, hugging her after the session.

"Thanks. I wanna get much better at jumping. And soon." Heather had to look down at the ice to make sure she wasn't walking on air!

Coach Sterling was nodding and rummaging around in his coat pocket. "Here, Miss Heather," he said, handing her a business card. "Give me a call when you want to get together again."

Heather could hardly stand still. "Mom?" she pleaded. "Can we make another appointment? *Please?*"

"Absolutely," Mom said, taking the card from Heather. "How about this Wednesday and Friday mornings?"

Mr. Sterling wrote in his pocket notebook. "I'll see you soon, Heather."

She walked to the mall entrance with Livvy. "Thanks for everything, Liv."

Livvy frowned, shaking her head. "You did all the work. I'm super proud of you!"

"You shared your coach with me, and I'm so excited," Heather replied, waiting for her mother to catch up.

"The sky's the limit now," Livvy told her. "Someday we'll be in the same competitions."

Heather hadn't thought of that. "Wow—that's hard to believe."

Livvy's eyes danced. "You've got what it takes. Coach Sterling wouldn't be offering you lessons if he didn't think so."

"You're probably right."

"Well, I better get going," Livvy said. "Coach'll be waiting. I'll see you at ballet."

"Okay. Thanks again!" Heather held the door for her mom, and the two of them walked to the car. "Thanks for believing in me. You don't know how happy I am."

"I think I do. Happiness is written all over your face."

Heather remembered what Kevin had said about her emotions showing on her face. He'd said, *"It's easy to read you."*

Well, for a change, she didn't mind. Not one bit! She was on her way to becoming a free skater. What had Livvy said about competing in the same events? Seemed next to impossible, but Heather thrived on a challenge.

"Are you coming to meet Cynthia Ganesford this afternoon?" Mom asked just as they pulled up to the house.

"I don't know. Kevin might not want me there."

Mom parked the car next to the sidewalk and pulled the key out of the ignition. "Well, I think you might be surprised."

"What're you saying?"

"Kevin asked if you'd come," Mom replied. "He wants you to meet Cynthia."

Heather wasn't sure how she felt about meeting her replacement. "I'll let you know after lunch."

"Okay with me."

They got out of the car and picked their way up the snowy front steps. All the while, Heather's thoughts were on her jumps. She had more important things to think about than Kevin's new ice-dancing partner. The way she felt now, she'd probably stay home. Let Mom and Coach McDonald do the audition. Wasn't her decision anyway.

CHAPTER 16

Mom and Kevin left at three o'clock to meet with Coach McDonald. They wanted to talk with him before Cynthia Ganesford showed up. Heather decided to skip the audition and stay home.

"Why didn't you go?" Joanne asked, plopping down next to Heather on the sofa.

"It's all up to Kevin now," she said, hugging a round pillow.

"But you *know* ice skating," her little sister insisted. "Maybe you could help Kevin decide if Cynthia's the right partner."

She turned to look at Joanne. Here was a first-grade munchkin far older than her years. And Joanne was probably right. She should've gone along.

But, no, it was much better this way. With all the talk of Cynthia, she didn't need to add her two cents. Besides, Kevin had already made up his mind. She was almost sure of it.

When the phone rang, Heather ignored it. She wasn't going to bother. She and Joanne were in a close game of tic-tac-toe.

"Aren't you gonna answer it?" Joanne asked.

"Don't feel like it," she said.

"Why not?"

"Just don't."

"Are you upset about Cynthia?" asked Joanne.

Heather frowned. "Why would you say a dumb thing like that?"

Joanne's eyes blinked rapidly, like she was in trouble. "Because I think it's true," she said softly.

The phone kept ringing.

Heather shook her head. "How could I be upset?" She wished Joanne hadn't brought this up. Not now.

"Because ice dancing is your life, and you know it." Joanne smashed her lips together, eyes wide. "I . . . I didn't mean to say that."

Standing up, Heather tossed the tic-tac-toe tablet onto her sister's lap. "I think you did mean it, and I'm outta here."

"Where are you going?" Joanne demanded.

"To my room."

The phone had stopped. And she could hear Joanne complaining about the unfinished game on the stairs. Closing her door, she wished she and Joanne hadn't fought. None of this stuff with Kevin and Cynthia was worth hard feelings in the family.

When she felt calmer, she went to her parents' bedroom

and phoned Livvy. "How was school?" she asked.

"I've got way too much homework," Livvy said. "I tried to call you earlier."

"Oh, was that you?"

"So you were busy or something?" Livvy asked.

"Yeah, with my little sister." She didn't want to say that she was bummed out in general. "What'd you call about?"

"I just happened to run into Kevin and your mom."

"You're kidding. How'd it go? With Cynthia, I mean."

Livvy paused for a second. "If I tell you, promise not to be upset?"

"How can I be upset? If my brother's found the perfect replacement, I'm thrilled. Case closed."

"She's an amazing skater, Heather. I watched them try out some dance steps and patterns. You should've been there to see it. I could hardly believe it was their first time on the ice together."

"That's definitely good news. Thanks for letting me know, Livvy."

Livvy talked about school and the outrageous amount of homework she already had for the week. But when Heather hung up, she hardly remembered much of anything Liv had said. Except for the report of Cynthia's *amazing* audition with Kevin.

During every minute of supper and dessert, her parents talked of nothing but Cynthia's performance. But it was

Kevin who beamed whenever the skater's name was mentioned.

He's nuts about her—on and off the ice, Heather decided. And the way she saw it, that alone was a problem. If Kevin really liked this girl, he'd be shy about putting his arm around her waist or holding her hand. There'd be no way he'd dance close to her on the ice, the way the judges required for good marks. Choosing a girl Kevin was attracted to was a big mistake.

But she wasn't going to intrude. If Kevin made a bad choice, he'd find out sooner or later. The first real practice session would tell him.

"It's for sure . . . about Cynthia, I mean?" she asked her mom in the kitchen during cleanup.

Mom poured detergent into the tiny cubicles in the door of the dishwasher. "Coach McDonald will be working with them in Colorado Springs next Saturday. We're going to take turns driving back and forth between there and here."

"Sounds like a good trade-off," she said. "Have you met her parents?"

"Very nice people," Mom replied. "Might even be Christians. But I guess we'll find out."

"That's great." She finished wiping the counters and dried a few pans that didn't fit into the dishwasher.

They had family devotions, and then Heather went to her room to work on unfinished schoolwork. Mom was a stickler about following through on things.

Ice dancing is your life. . . .

Joanne's childish words kept intruding into her thoughts off and on all evening. Not until she got wrapped up in a library book on free skating was Heather able to nudge the ridiculous assumption out of her mind.

CHAPTER 17

Making birthday party plans for her dad and practicing jumps consumed most of Heather's free time. There were occasional spats with Kevin, but they seemed to occur during homeschooling sessions. The disagreements had nothing to do with skating, either free skating or ice dancing. For the most part, their relationship was still intact.

By Wednesday, she found herself enthusiastic to work with Livvy's coach once again. Mr. Sterling was the most helpful, kind coach she'd ever known. Not any more than her former coach, of course, but he had a wonderfully encouraging way about him. Made you want to work till you dropped.

Livvy didn't show up for Heather's second jump lesson with Coach Sterling. Just as well. Heather wanted to make her own connection with the kindly gentleman.

"You are improving so rapidly, Miss Heather, you make my head spin," Coach Sterling told her after the lesson.

"Thank you very much." She could hardly wait to tell her parents. And Livvy, too.

The walk home seemed shorter than usual. Maybe it was because she was so jazzed up about her progress. Yet in spite of her development as a free skater, something seemed not quite right. Try as she might, she couldn't put her finger on it.

After the supper dishes were cleared from the table, she asked permission to use her father's computer. Checking her library book, she found a listing of the top-ten ice-skating Web sites.

In an instant, she located the Kristi Yamaguchi Web page and info about the Stars on Ice tour and other skating news. There were many Internet links to figure-skating tidbits and bios of the most famous free skaters in the world. For an hour, she was lost in a world of extraordinary people—brilliant skaters and lavish costumes.

Lying in bed, her head buzzed with high hopes of becoming a Junior Olympics gold medalist. Her focus, hard work, and determination would get her where she wanted to be.

Had to!

On Thursday morning, she went to the mall rink to practice. Kevin did the same. In fact, they shared the ice, but not their practice. It seemed terribly odd to Heather, and she did her best not to keep watching her brother. But it was hard to focus on her own work.

Kevin worked through his solo stroking as usual, then went right into his half of the cha-cha dance pattern. She tried to ignore his marvelous, intricate footwork and turns. Of course, the only thing missing was his partner.

Heather busied herself with preparations for the flip and Lutz jumps. The setup for the Lutz had her stumped nearly every time. Skating backward in a curve—and the long glide into the jump—was definitely difficult.

Once, when she fell, she felt stunned for a moment. Both Mom and Kevin came running. But it was Kevin who picked her up gently and held on to her while she got her bearings again.

"Maybe you oughta take a break for a while," he said, guiding her off the ice.

"I'm fine," she said. "Thanks."

He stood there, looking down at her. "You sure you're all right?"

She nodded, waiting till he'd turned and stepped back onto the ice to rub her leg.

"Are you hurt, honey?" Mom asked, hovering over her.

"Just a little bruised, that's all."

"Maybe Kevin's right about taking it easy. You've been pushing yourself really hard these days." Mom sat beside her, looking on with sympathetic eyes.

"I can't slow down, Mom. You know I can't." She sighed. "I'm so far behind."

Mom patted her hand. They stared out at the ice—at

Kevin executing one beautiful dance pattern after another.
Alone.

Heather sat on a soft chair in Jenna's bedroom later that
afternoon. Her leg still hurt from her reckless fall, so Jenna
and Livvy babied her by giving her the chair. Actually, she
was hurting in two places. Her leg hurt because she'd
pushed herself too hard at practice. The second hurt was
deep in the core of her stomach. The pain wasn't a typical
stomachache—like from something she'd eaten or the flu.
Nothing like that. The ache was more like the squeamish,
worrisome feeling she often experienced before an ice-
dancing competition. But she knew that was ridiculous.
There were no events coming up very soon. This was mid-
January. The next big event was the Summer Ice Spectacular.

Oops . . . she'd forgotten. She almost laughed out loud.
Once again she was thinking about her former interest. Ice
dancing was none of her concern. She was something else
now. A free skater with the brightest future ever.

Why do I feel so miserable? she wondered.

The pain in her stomach didn't go away. Not even when
the *Girls Only* club was called to order. There was no following the bylaws this meeting. And Miranda Garcia was the
reason. She had asked if it was possible to have the meeting
a day earlier this week because she was already busy during
their normal Friday meeting. Jenna, the prez, wanted to

make sure their ballet friend was comfortable. So they threw out the rule book and just had a good time chattering about school and boys . . . and of course, sports.

When they went to the barre and warmed up, she partnered with Livvy. Jenna put on a CD of Chopin waltzes, and Heather began to relax.

Halfway through the stretches, she started to laugh. She couldn't stop, either. Livvy, not knowing what was so funny, began to laugh, too.

At that moment—sharing the barre with Livvy—Heather realized what was causing the pain in her stomach. She missed her partner. In spite of her longings, she honestly wanted things to return to the way they had been. Before she'd decided to go it alone. Before she'd given up the best partner ever. "I have to talk to my brother," she said through her laughter.

Livvy was nodding. "It's about ice dancing, isn't it?"

Heather pulled herself up to a standing position. "How'd you know?"

Livvy grinned and tossed her hair. "Just guessed."

They fell into each other's arms. Giggles spilled over into the attic bedroom-turned-clubhouse. Jenna turned up the volume on the Chopin, while Miranda kept at her warm-ups.

"Are the meetings always this wacky and wonderful?" asked Miranda over raspberry lemonade.

"Pretty much," Jenna said, smiling. "Wanna see a teeny, weenie gymnast?"

"Sure do," Miranda said.

Jenna said, "Follow me," and the three of them headed

for the nursery to see the amazing left foot of baby Jonathan.

The club meeting ended with a swing dance run-through. "The choreography was created by none other than Heather Bock!" Jenna announced.

"Go, girl!" Miranda said, thumbs up.

Once again, Heather teamed up with Livvy for the practice. While she danced with her partner, the pain in the pit of her stomach began to disappear. And soon, it was completely gone.

Now, how to break her news to Kevin. Was it too late?

CHAPTER 18

Heather had a tough time finding Kevin alone without either Joanne or Tommy hanging around. What she had to tell him might change their travel plans tomorrow. Might change both their athletic futures, too.

Finally, after family devotions, she nabbed him. "I need to talk to you," she said, cornering him in the upstairs hallway.

"Sure, what's up?" His eyes seemed to look through to her heart.

"You won't yell at me, will you?"

He looked thoroughly confused. "About what?"

"About me not wanting to skate solo." There, she'd said it. Now what would he do?

His face lit into a smile. "What did you just say?"

"I said I miss skating with you. I . . . I made a big mistake." Tears were stinging her eyes. "I was crazy to give up everything we'd ever worked for."

Kevin put his arms around her and patted her head. "You're crazy, little sister."

"Will you let me skate with you again?" she sobbed into his old flannel shirt.

"On one condition," he said, holding her at arm's length. "Are you through with free skating?"

"Do I look like Kristi Yamaguchi to you?" She spun around in front of him, bursting into laughter.

"Man, will Mom be shocked," Kevin said, pulling her arm and racing down the stairs. "But it'll work out. You'll see."

Leave it to Kevin to be optimistic at a time like this. No matter what, though, Heather knew she could count on her partner.

"What about Cynthia?" she said as they hurried to the kitchen.

"What *about* her?" He was laughing, too. "I've got the perfect partner right here."

No matter what she might've thought about other days in her life, this day—this moment—was the very best of all.

Definitely.

Don't miss GIRLS ONLY *(GO!)* #4!

Reach for the Stars

Miranda Garcia is training for the Dressel Hills Downhill Classic when her single mother, a ski instructor, breaks her leg on the slope. Miranda takes over her mother's four- to six-year-old beginner's group and meets a precocious boy named Tarin Greenberg, aka "Tarin the Terrible."

When Tarin's father, who is also single, wants to interview Miranda for a baby-sitting job, her friends in the Girls Only Club warn her not to take the job because of some curious information they know about the situation. But Miranda's motivation for taking the job is more than just money. She feels drawn to Mr. Greenberg because of a renewed longing for her own father, who abandoned the family years ago. With the help of the other girls, Miranda devises a plan to introduce Mr. Greenberg to Miranda's mother. Will the two hit it off, or has Miranda made a huge mistake?

Also by Beverly Lewis

PICTURE BOOK

Cows in the House

THE CUL-DE-SAC KIDS
Children's Fiction

The Double Dabble Surprise   *Fiddlesticks*
The Chicken Pox Panic   *The Crabby Cat Caper*
The Crazy Christmas Angel Mystery   *Tarantula Toes*
No Grown-ups Allowed   *Green Gravy*
Frog Power   *Backyard Bandit Mystery*
The Mystery of Case D. Luc   *Tree House Trouble*
The Stinky Sneakers Mystery   *The Creepy Sleep-Over*
Pickle Pizza   *The Great TV Turn-Off*
Mailbox Mania   *Piggy Party*
The Mudhole Mystery   *The Granny Game*

SUMMERHILL SECRETS
Youth Fiction

Whispers Down the Lane   *A Cry in the Dark*
Secret in the Willows   *House of Secrets*
Catch a Falling Star   *Echoes in the Wind*
Night of the Fireflies   *Hide Behind the Moon*
Windows on the Hill

HOLLY'S HEART SERIES
Youth Fiction

Holly's First Love   *Straight-A Teacher*
Secret Summer Dreams   *The "No-Guys" Pact*
Sealed With a Kiss   *Little White Lies*
The Trouble With Weddings   *Freshmen Frenzy*
California Christmas   *Mystery Letters*
Second-Best Friend   *Eight Is Enough*
Good-bye, Dressel Hills   *It's a Girl Thing*

THE HERITAGE OF LANCASTER COUNTY
Adult Fiction

The Shunning   *The Confession*
The Reckoning

GIFT BOOK

The Sunroom

Series for Middle Graders* From BHP

ADVENTURES DOWN UNDER · by Robert Elmer
When Patrick McWaid's father is unjustly sent to Australia as a prisoner in 1867, the rest of the family follows, uncovering action-packed mystery along the way.

ADVENTURES OF THE NORTHWOODS · by Lois Walfrid Johnson
Kate O'Connell and her stepbrother Anders encounter mystery and adventure in northwest Wisconsin near the turn of the century.

AN AMERICAN ADVENTURE SERIES · by Lee Roddy
Hildy Corrigan and her family must overcome danger and hardship during the Great Depression as they search for a "forever home."

BLOODHOUNDS, INC. · by Bill Myers
Hilarious, hair-raising suspense follows brother-and-sister detectives Sean and Melissa Hunter in these madcap mysteries with a message.

GIRLS ONLY! · by Beverly Lewis
Four talented young athletes become fast friends as together they pursue their Olympic dreams.

JOURNEYS TO FAYRAH · by Bill Myers
Join Denise, Nathan, and Josh on amazing journeys as they discover the wonders and lessons of the mystical Kingdom of Fayrah.

MANDIE BOOKS · by Lois Gladys Leppard
With over four million sold, the turn-of-the-century adventures of Mandie and her many friends will keep readers eager for more.

THE RIVERBOAT ADVENTURES · by Lois Walfrid Johnson
Libby Norstad and her friend Caleb face the challenges and risks of working with the Underground Railroad during the mid–1800s.

TRAILBLAZER BOOKS · by Dave and Neta Jackson
Follow the exciting lives of real-life Christian heroes through the eyes of child characters as they share their faith with others around the world.

THE TWELVE CANDLES CLUB · by Elaine L. Schulte
When four twelve-year-old girls set up a business of odd jobs and baby-sitting, they uncover wacky adventures and hilarious surprises.

THE YOUNG UNDERGROUND · by Robert Elmer
Peter and Elise Andersen's plots to protect their friends and themselves from Nazi soldiers in World War II Denmark guarantee fast-paced action and suspenseful reads.

*(ages 8–13)